MY PEACE
By Courtney Cole

A Pax Tate novel
(The Beautifully Broken series)

Happy endings must be worked for.

Courtney Cole

My Peace

Courtney Cole

Lakehouse Press, Inc.

This book is an original publication of Lakehouse Press, Inc.
All rights reserved.

No part of this book may be reproduced, scanned, or distributed in any printed or electronic forms without permission. Please do not participate in or encourage piracy of copyrighted materials in violation of this author's rights. Purchase only authorized editions.

This book is a work of fiction. Names, characters, places and incidents are either the product of the author's imagination or are used fictitiously and any resemblance to a person, alive or dead, business establishments, events or locales, is purely coincidental.

Copyright © 2017, Courtney Cole

Library of Congress Cataloging-in-publication data

Cole, Courtney
My Peace/Courtney Cole/Lakehouse Press Inc/Trade pbk ed

ISBN 13: 978-1542483766

ISNB 10: 154248376X

Printed in the United States of America

MY PEACE

Prologue

I am flat on my back, I think.

It's hard to say, because I feel like I'm floating. Through space, through water, through something.

I'm the perfect temperature. Not hot, not cold.

Nothing bothers me here, not in this abyss. Worries, stress, reality. All are gone. Far from me, far from here.

I can't feel.

I can't think.

I don't need to.

Still, even though it's perfect here, and black and void, something isn't right. I know that. It niggles at me, bothering me, like an itch. I scratch at it, at the thought, and I realize that it bothers me because I shouldn't be here.

This is an old familiar place, a place I haven't visited in a long time.

Oblivion.

How did I get here?

What the fuck happened?

I furrow my brow and try to think…

Chapter One

Pax

Pushing back from my desk, I stretch, arching my back and flexing my arms.

My leather shoes squeak when I move, and my toes are confined.

I fucking hate wearing suits.

Glancing at my watch, I realize the time.

"Damn it." I grab the phone and punch the button for my assistant.

"Yes, Mr. Tate?"

"Would you call my car for me? I'm late."

"Yes, sir."

I don't bother reminding her that she doesn't need to call me *sir*. Sasha was my grandfather's assistant before he retired, and he was old-school. Old habits die hard for her.

As I stride through my office doors, Sasha scrambles to her feet at her desk.

"Here's your bag," she thrusts it into my hands. "But what should I tell Mr. Andre? You had a meeting with him tonight to discuss a proposal."

"Fuck," I mutter. "I forgot. Can you reschedule for tomorrow? I've got somewhere important to be."

"Of course. Have a good night, sir."

"You, too."

When I reach the street, the doorman opens the door for me, and my car is waiting, a long sleek, black Cadillac. It was also inherited from my grandfather. He believed that

MY PEACE

the CEO of Alexander Holdings should arrive and depart from work in a chauffeured car. He was, and still is, a big believer in creating your own reality.

If we portray a sense of success, we will be successful.

We already are, and we don't need to put on a show to prove it, but I grudgingly agreed to his quirks when I took over for him two years ago. "I need to get to the Minnow, Rog," I tell the driver. "I'm late."

"Will do." He takes off like a bullet, and I go about the impossible task of changing my clothes in the backseat of a moving car.

My legs are long, so folding and contorting myself to change clothes must look ridiculous. I see Roger's lip twitch in the rearview mirror.

"Shut it," I growl at him, shoving my arm into a black t-shirt sleeve. I lift my hips and wiggle into my favorite jeans, and thankfully, finally, replace my loafers with broken-in cowboy boots.

"Ahh," I sigh, settling back into the seat. "That's more like it."

I'm comfortable in jeans and a tee. It's where I belong. It's much easier to swallow being driven around when you're wearing comfortable clothes.

I grab my phone and text my wife.
Babe, I'll be there in 5.
There are three bubbles.
Hurry up. I miss you.
I smile. *I'm coming.*
Three bubbles. *You wish.*

I laugh now, and this is my favorite part of my day… when I get to see Mila. She's just the right combination of sassy and sweet, sexy and innocent. She's perfect, and deep down, I know I don't deserve her. But she's stayed with me anyway.

Soon, the car glides up to the curb in front of the Wounded Minnow, and I get out.

"You don't need to wait. I'll drive home with my wife."

Roger nods. "Have a good night, boss."

"You, too."

I push through the front door of the bar, and search the crowded room. Mila stands up at a booth in the back and her face lights up when she smiles, her green eyes bright.

She's with her sister and brother-in-law, Madison and Gabe. They all wave, and I weave through the crowded room to get to them. When I do, Mila stands up on her tiptoes to kiss me, her soft lips pressed to mine. She smells like lavender and vanilla, like all things good in the world.

She smells like home.

"Hey, babe," I murmur against her lips, and my hands stretch around to press her hips into mine. "I missed you."

"I missed you, too," she answers, and she wiggles up against me.

"God, get a room," Madison groans from the table, and we break apart, laughing.

"It's not my fault that your husband is too tired to..."

"Watch it," Gabe interrupts me, glaring over his whiskey glass. "When you have a two-month old again, one who doesn't want to sleep, you can give me shit about being tired. Until then, bite me."

His eyes are red, there are bags under them, and the whole thing cracks me up.

"Odd that Maddy looks as gorgeous as usual," I point out, sliding into the booth and kissing my sister-in-law on the cheek. She really does look gorgeous, tall and blonde. She is the polar opposite of my wife, who is petite and brunette. But they are both beautiful.

"Flattery gets you everywhere," Maddy promises me, and she signals for the bartender. "He needs a drink," she announces to him.

"Just club soda," I tell him.

Maddy rolls her eyes. "You can let loose tonight," she tells me. "We're celebrating."

"What exactly are we celebrating?" I ask as Mila settles into the crook of my arm, her hand on my thigh. Her fingers slide upward a little, toward my groin, and I give her side-eye. The evil minx grins from ear to ear.

"You know… your contract with Defense Tech," Mila reminds me, as though her fingers aren't a quarter of an inch from my penis.

I swallow. "Oh, yes. Another year of me keeping Gabe in a job."

Gabe cackles, and rolls his eyes because it's not true and we both know it. His business has grown exponentially, and without my business, his body armor company would still be fine. I did give him his start, though. And I'm never one to pass up taking credit for something.

"Whatever," he grunts. "You're lucky to have me and you know it, dude."

We laugh and chat for the next hour, and it feels so fucking good to be sitting around a table in a dingy little bar with the people I love the most.

"How was ZuZu today?" I ask my wife.

"Same as when you left this morning. Four going on fourteen."

"That's my girl," I grin.

"I'm still pissed that you aren't calling her Maddy," Madison complains. "You named her after me. I feel cheated."

"Whatever," Mila tells her. "It got confusing and you know it."

"Yeah, but to nickname her after the girl in A Wonderful Life? That movie is just depressing," she complains again. "Seriously."

"It is not," Mila defends us. "And it's also after her middle name, Susanna. ZuZu is a fitting name. So hush."

Maddy rolls her eyes, but my daughter has her wrapped around her little pinkie and we all know it. Maddy has bought her approximately one hundred pairs of shoes in this year alone.

I start to mention it, but Maddy holds up her hand. "She needed those pink cowboy boots."

I snort. "What about the other ninety-nine pairs?"

"That's neither here nor there," Maddy sniffs.

Mila laughs and signals the waiter for another glass of wine. "You want a glass, honey?" she asks me.

"Sure. One glass won't hurt anything."

Maddy sighs from across the table. "You've got such willpower, Pax."

"And to think, you used to think I was a lost cause," I rib her.

"I did," she admits without remorse. "But you proved us all wrong."

"Yup."

We order big juicy burgers, and Mila and I sip at our wine while Maddy and Gabe play a game of pool. Mila nestles in the crook of my shoulder, and I run my fingers through the tips of her dark hair.

"Did you have a good day?" I ask and her fingers curl around my arm.

"Yes. It's better now, though."

I smile, kissing the top of her head.

"Yeah."

"How was work?"

I growl lightly. "Nope. No work talk. I'm out of that suit and I'm here with you."

Mila smiles. "I don't think you dislike it nearly as much as you say."

I think on that. I don't dislike the respect that the job commands. I don't dislike the salary, although, since I've always had a trust fund, the money wasn't new to me.

"I guess I just hate the confinement," I admit. "I hate the suits. And the *Yes, sirs.* It doesn't feel like me."

"It's *not* you," Mila agrees. "It's just your job. You can be you again when you come home. But you're so good at what you do. Your grandfather was just telling me so the other day."

I can't help but feel satisfaction in that, in his approval. William Alexander is hard to impress, and once you've done it, you don't forget it.

"Good."

"He's coming over for dinner next week," she mentions. I nod.

"Ok."

The heat from Mila's body is comforting, and we are spooned together as much as we can be in a bar booth. Mila lifts her head from my chest. "I'm ready to go home now," she tells me softly. Her eyes are large and suggestive.

"Any particular reason why?" I ask, my eyebrow raised.

"I'll give you three guesses," she answers, sliding her hand discreetly up my thigh again.

I catch her fingers deftly.

"Ok. Let's get you out of here before you get us arrested for indecent exposure."

She giggles and we head to the pool table to say our goodnights. We leave Madison winning at pool and Gabe desperately trying to pretend he's losing on purpose. We all know better. He's a big bad Army Ranger, but Madison doesn't lose at anything she puts her mind to.

We walk through the dark parking lot to my wife's SUV. I open the passenger door and help her in, and when I get in the driver's side, I'm assaulted immediately by my wife.

She presses against me, her lips against mine, her tongue plunging into my mouth.

"I've *really* missed you," she says softly, her hand splayed against my chest.

"I've only been gone eight hours," I tell her, but I'm not very convincing, because I missed her too.

"We're pathetic," she points out, but she doesn't care and neither do I.

"We're *lucky*," I correct her, as I stroke my fingers against her. She arches into my hand.

"Very lucky. And you're about to get luckier."

She unfastens my pants and dips her head, and before I know it, my wife is giving me a blowjob in the parking lot.

I suck in a breath as her fingers curl around my balls, just like I'd taught her years ago.

"Fuck," I exhale.

"In a minute," Mila agrees, her mouth against my shaft.

She slides her lips up and down, and the suction… Lord have mercy.

"You're killing me, woman," I groan. She grins, and I lift her onto my lap.

She pulls her panties down.

I can't breathe.

She grins again.

Then I plunge into her, using my arms to lift her up… then down.

"Christ."

"Yeah," she sighs against my neck.

The thrill of making love to my wife in a public place, where anyone might happen upon us, is exhilarating.

I only last a few minutes longer because of it, and soon, I'm spasming inside of her, wet and hot.

She clutches at my hair when she finds her own release.

"Pax," she sighs. "Pax."

"That's it, baby," I rock with her, feeling her shudder around me. "Let it go."

I hold her tight for a few more minutes, her hair plastered to her forehead, and sticking to my chest.

"That was nice," she says sleepily.

"That was fantastic," I correct. "But I need to get you home to our bed."

She nods in agreement, and we put our clothes back on. Mila straps into the passenger seat, and I nose the SUV out of the parking spot and then out of the lot toward home.

Hartford is dark and quiet at this time of night, and traffic is light. It's an easy drive, and I settle in for it, turning the radio on low.

Mila is asleep within five minutes, and I glance over at her.

Her hair is falling across her cheek, and her hand is curled under her chin. She looks angelic. No one would ever guess what we had just done in a public parking lot.

I turn onto the street that leads up to our subdivision, and our headlights shine onto a car pulled over onto the shoulder.

A woman stands next to it, studying her flat tire with a perplexed look on her face.

I can't just drive past.

It's midnight, and the woman is alone. It wouldn't be right.

So, I pull up behind her.

Mila stirs.

"I'll just be a minute," I tell her. "Someone has car trouble."

She murmurs a response, and I step into the brisk night air.

"Do you have a spare?" I call out as I walk toward the woman. She's startled, but then smiles.

"Um. I'm not sure," she answers sheepishly. "I've never had a flat before."

"Well, don't worry. I can help," I assure her. "Can you pop your trunk?"

She gets in her car and finds the button, and I hear the thump of the trunk's lever releasing. I turn to walk to it, and headlights are suddenly in my face.

Not my own headlights.

MY PEACE

In this moment, I know how a deer must feel, because it's disorienting, and I'm not sure which way to move, and then the decision is made for me.

Something slams into me and I'm hurtling through the air.

My last conscious thought is... *Jesus, this should hurt, but it doesn't.*

And then everything is black.

Chapter Two

Mila

Sweet Lord, I can't believe we're here again.

I'm pacing the hospital waiting room, and Pax is behind the double doors, and I don't know what's happening.

"M'am, did you get a look at the vehicle?" The policeman in front of me tries to keep me on track, when all I want to do is barge through the doors and find my husband.

"No," I tell him again, for the fifth time. "I'm sorry. I was half-asleep and my eyes were closed."

I feel guilty about that now. I mean, my husband was trying to help someone and I couldn't be bothered to wake up?

"Stop it," my sister says, eyeing me. She knows me too well. "This wasn't your fault."

"I know," I mumble. "It was an accident." I look up at her. "Can you call Chelcie, and ask her to stay the night with Zu? I don't know what time I'll be leaving here."

Maddy nods. "Of course." She disappears around a corner as she pulls her phone out of her purse to call my babysitter, and Gabe falls into step with me as I pace. His big body dwarfs mine, the skull-and-crossbones tattoo on his bicep reading *death before dishonor.*

"You don't have to babysit me," I tell him. "I'm fine."

MY PEACE

"I'm not babysitting," he protests. "I'm pacing. I like to pace."

He stays in step with me for a few minutes more before he speaks again.

"He's going to be fine, Mila."

I nod, because there's no way he'll be anything else. Pax is strong, he's a fighter. He's overcome so much already.

The policeman clears his throat, and I had almost forgotten he was here.

"If you are contacted by anyone, by the girl you stopped to help, for example, will you let us know?'

He offers me his card and I take it, and I'm confused.

"Wait. You haven't spoken with the girl?"

The policeman eyes me. "No. As I mentioned earlier, she left the scene."

I don't remember that at all. "I'm sorry," I tell him. "I'm a bit flustered."

He nods. "It's perfectly understandable. Just let us know if, for some reason, she tries to contact you."

"Ok."

He leaves, and Gabe and I pace together for a few more minutes. Finally, I'm too tired to pace, and I collapse into a chair. Maddy comes back, and holds my hand, and I'm just closing my eyes to rest them when the surgeon emerges from the door.

I know it's the surgeon because he's wearing one of those caps that you see on ER shows, and he looks exhausted.

"Your husband is going to be ok," he tells me quietly. Gabe, Maddy and I exhale collectively, a mass release of pent-up anxiety. "His spleen was ruptured in the impact, but we've removed it and stopped the internal bleeding. His knee was hyper-extended, as well. He'll be sore, but he's going to make it."

If I weren't already sitting, I would collapse from relief. My knees feel numb.

"Can I see him?" I ask quickly.

"Yes. I'll have a nurse come get you when he's wheeled to a room." He disappears back through the doors and Maddy hugs me tightly.

"See? I told you."

I nod, and I'm still numb. "Yeah."

It's not very long until a nurse comes to get me, and takes me to Pax.

I pause at the door, looking at the man in the bed.

He's paler than he should be, he's got tubes hooked up to his hand, and he's got muscles and tattoos. He's mine, although being here, reminds me of a night when he wasn't mine yet. The night I first met him.

He'd overdosed on the beach, and I'd found him in a pool of vomit. I'd given him CPR and called an ambulance, and then had come to see him the next day in the hospital. I might've fallen in love with him that very day.

His hazel eyes open now, slowly, but they brighten when he sees me.

"Hey, Red," he says softly. "What took you so long?"

I laugh, because I'm his little Red Riding Hood and he's my Big Bad Wolf. Always and forever. I rush across the room, and grab his hand, the one that doesn't have an IV.

"Oh my God, you scared me," I breathe, inhaling his neck, and kissing his cheek. "Sweet Lord, Pax."

MY PEACE

"You scare easily," he points out, and his arm wraps around me, tugging me closer.

"No," I answer firmly. "*You got hit by a car.* A car."

"We don't know for sure it's a car," he replies. "It could've been a truck. Or an SUV. It sorta felt like an SUV."

He rubs at his hip, and I roll my eyes to hide my panic.

"You're ridiculous," I tell him.

He grins.

"Yeah. But you love me."

"Yeah."

Pax tugs me until I tumble over the bed railing and collapse into his side. I snuggle there, into his arm, and he smells unfamiliar, like iodine and sterility. Not like my Pax.

"You stink," I mumble into his arm.

He chuckles.

"You don't." He sniffs at my hair. "You always smell the same. Like Lavender and vanilla. You're my home, babe."

"The drugs have you addled," I tell him, but his words warm my heart. They almost make all of the panic and anxiety worth it. Almost. "Did you know the girl?" I ask. "The police said she left the scene."

I feel my husband shake his head. "Nope. She was just a random chick with a flat tire. She didn't know how to change it."

"Then how did she flee the scene?" I wonder aloud.

Pax shrugs. "She was probably freaked out and drove on the rim. Who knows?"

"We'll never know," I agree. "All that matters is that you're going to be ok."

"You should go home and get some rest," Pax tells me. "Seriously. I'll be ok, sweetheart."

My gut clenches, because God. If the car or truck or SUV, or whatever the hell it was, had been just one more inch to the right, Pax wouldn't have been so lucky. It makes me sick to my stomach and I clench his hand tightly.

"No. I'm staying right here."

"But what about Zu?"

"I had Maddy call Chelcie."

"Babe, go home. Just come back in the morning. You won't be able to sleep here."

I'm trying to protest when a nurse interrupts us. "Yes, Mrs. Tate. You really can't be here tonight. He's in recovery, and I need to monitor his vitals. I'm not sure I'll get an accurate pulse read if you are in bed with him." She gestures toward the monitors with a wry smile, and Pax laughs.

"True," he points out. "You affect me, Red."

"Still?" I ask breathlessly, and he grins again.

"Do you really doubt that?"

I shake my head, remembering what we had done in the parking lot earlier. "No."

"Good. Go home. Give Zu a kiss for me, and come back in the morning to get me."

"I doubt you'll be ready for release that soon," the nurse cautions him, but Pax ignores her.

"I'll call Roger," Pax reaches for his phone, but I shake my head.

"No. It's the middle of the night. I'll have Gabe drop me off."

"They're still here?" Pax lifts an eyebrow.

MY PEACE

"Of course. They love you. They'll take me to get our car tomorrow, too."

He nods and I throw my arms around his neck. He winces, then hides it.

"Are your pain meds wearing off?" I ask, then I turn to the nurse before he answers. "He needs more. Please don't let him be in pain."

"He's in good hands," she assures me. "I promise."

"Ok."

Pax kisses my lips softly, and then a little more insistently. The nurse clears her throat, gesturing again at the monitor. I smile against my husband's lips.

"I guess I do affect you," I sigh. "I'll be back in the morning. Don't go anywhere."

He chuckles, and I get up, but I pause at the door.

The nurse is checking the pulse at his wrist, and he's so big and strong, and he looks so out of place in the hospital bed.

"I love you," I tell him.

His eyes are gold as he looks up at me. "I love you, too, Red. Sweet dreams."

"Always."

I force myself to leave, and Gabe and Maddy walk me through the hospital corridors and out into the chilly night.

I'm silent as they drive me home, my eyes hot and red from lack of sleep.

"He's ok," my sister reminds me as we pull into my driveway. "You can relax and get some sleep."

"I know," I agree. "Thank you for giving me a ride."

"We'll be back in the morning to take you to your car," Gabe says gruffly.

"Thank you, guys," I murmur as I climb out. "Really."

They wait as I unlock the door, and then they drive away, their taillights disappearing into the night.

I glance at my watch. It's three-thirty a.am.

Chelcie is asleep on the sofa and I hesitate to wake her.

"I'm home," I tell her softly. "Feel free to stay here tonight, if you'd like."

"Is Pax ok?" she asks worriedly, sitting up. I nod. I know she's sincerely concerned. She's like family now. She was our waitress over a year ago in a tiny dive café, and after talking with her, we found out that she was an orphan, that she had no money, and she was trying to put herself through college.

That was all it took. Pax paid her tuition the next day, and she's been our babysitter ever since.

"He's fine," I tell her. "His spleen ruptured, so they had to take it out. He'll be in the hospital overnight, but he's fine."

"Oh my God," she breathes, and her eyes are huge. "I can't believe it. Did they catch the guy?"

"No. Not yet. It was a hit and run."

"Jesus," she breathes, pulling off her blanket. "What can I do?"

"You've already done it," I tell her. "You stayed here with Zu. Thank you, Chelcie. I mean it."

"Anytime. Of course."

She rubs at her eyes and I glance around the room. It's large, comfortable, and nice. It's not over-the-top fancy, because Pax and I aren't like that. But the furnishings are expensive, tasteful and classic. Our house is large, but it's still homey.

"Zuzu is sleeping," Chelcie adds needlessly. "She went to bed at nine, and she's been asleep ever since."

MY PEACE

"Thanks, Chels. You can stay in the guest room, if you want. You probably shouldn't drive so late."

She shakes her head. "I'm fine. I've got an exam at eight, so I should go."

"Ok." I walk her to the door, and when she's gone, I set the alarm. We live in a nice neighborhood, but I've always been careful. Maddy says I'm paranoid, but it's not that. I'm just realistic.

After finding out that Pax's mother had been murdered in cold blood so long ago by their mailman, I've learned that life can be tragic and random, and it's smart to be cautious. People can be sick, and you never know what a person is *really* like until you truly get to know them.

I strip off my clothes and brush my teeth and climb into our giant bed alone.

With only me in it, it is enormous, and Pax's side is cold.

I stare out the wall of windows facing me, at the view of the gardens. I watch the treetops sway in the night, and I know that in a couple of hours, the sun will come up, and when it does, when the first fingers of dawn stretch into my daughter's room, Zuzu will be wide awake.

My phone buzzes on my nightstand.

Go to sleep. I love you.

I smile at my husband's text. He knows me well.

Quit being bossy, I answer. *But I love you, too.*

Across town, Pax is lying awake in a hospital bed, and he's just as unable to sleep as I am, because we're so used to falling asleep entwined together.

I'll see you soon, I add.

Closing my eyes, I let the darkness swallow me up, enveloping me in its silent void.

Sleep comes quickly.

MY PEACE

Chapter Three

Pax

I groan as I move.

"Son of a bitch," I mutter, as I attempt to get dressed. My fucking back feels like it was twisted into a pretzel and then chewed on by iron teeth. I groan again, and the young nurse walking in notices.

"You ok?" she raises an eyebrow, her dark eyes showing concern. "I don't think you should've signed yourself out."

"I've got things to do," I tell her. "And being here isn't going to help anything."

"You could rest here," she makes her way across the room, and stops next to me, her hands on my shoulders. She palpates my tender body, feeling for… I don't know what. Her fingers linger on my chest. "I would take very good care of you."

I'm startled because her tone has just gotten very suggestive and I know I'm not imagining it.

She smiles slightly, and I move away, out of her reach.

"That's ok," I tell her firmly. "My wife will take good care of me at home."

The nurse isn't bothered. "She's not trained like I am," she points out, and she turns off the monitors, and bends slowly in front of me to straighten the pillow that I'm not even using. Her ass is in the air in front of me. "I know exactly what I'm doing."

Holy shit.

"How unprofessional," I say. I'm not harsh, and I'm not mean, but there's one thing I've learned in life. You have to be direct for people to understand you.

She pauses, assessing me, assessing my interest.

When she sees that I'm not interested, at all, she straightens and is back to business, pretending that she hadn't spoken.

She hands me a paper. "These are your discharge instructions," she says, and she's perfunctory now. "You need to follow up with your physician, you should avoid physical activity until your doctor clears you. Take it easy because you're going to be sore for a while. Here is a script for pain medication. Because of your history, they are non-narcotic, but they will still help. You're going to need them. You're pretty banged up."

"You think?" I ask dryly, wincing again as I move.

"Don't try to be a tough guy," she advises. "You need to stay in front of the pain. So if the instructions say take two every four hours, do it."

I nod. "Fine. Thank you."

She pauses at the door, and looks at me one more time. "Do you need anything else?"

She appears to be hopeful. Jesus.

"No, thanks," I tell her.

"Well, if you change your mind, press the 'call' button."

She disappears and I exhale. Is that what women are like nowadays? I've been off the market for five years, but I swear, some women see a wedding ring as a challenge.

I am quickly distracted though, because I hear the thud of small sneakered feet and then girlish shrieks.

"Daddy!" Zuzu bounds into the room, her blond curls bouncing as she leaps up next to me. I swallow hard from being jostled.

"Punkin," I hug her with one arm, and she smells like sunshine and little girl. "I missed you."

She looks up at me with green eyes just like her mama's. "Mommy says you hurt yourself."

"Well, yeah. I guess I did. But I'm ok," I assure her.

Mila steps into the room. "If you'd stop stepping in front of moving vehicles, you'd be perfect."

I chuckle. "I hope you're here to spring me out."

"Only if you promise to be a good boy," she says sassily, and her eye gleam as she approaches. "Be careful with daddy," she tells Zu. "He's fragile."

I roll my eyes and heft myself up. "I'll show you fragile," I grumble under my breath. My wife just laughs.

"You ready to go home?" she asks, her eyebrow raised. "Or were you wanting to sleep here another night?"

"Let's get the f…" I pause, eying my daughter. "Flock out."

My daughter leads the way, skipping down the corridor, making nurses smile at her. Every step I take hurts like hell, but I try not to show it. I'm not a pussy, and I'm not going to act like one.

Once we're loaded into Mila's SUV, she glances at me. "I'll go get your meds after I get you home. I don't want you to have to wait at the pharmacy."

"I'm not an invalid," I tell her, but Jesus, the seat makes my back scream. Every muscle in my body feels like it is contracting, twisting, and has been shredded though a meat grinder.

"No arguments," Mila says firmly as she pulls out of the parking space and onto the road. "You're my patient now, and I'm a strict nurse. Some might even say militant."

"You'd better listen, daddy," Zuzu advises from the backseat. "Momma knows everything."

I raise an eyebrow, even though that hurts, too. "Everything?"

Zu nods. "Yup."

"Listen to your daughter," Mila laughs. "She's wise. She gets that from me."

We drive over a bump and I suck in a breath as the pain reverberates through my ribcage. Mila glances at me.

"How bad is it?" she asks.

"Not at all," I lie. "It's great. Refreshing, actually."

My wife rolls her eyes. "Reminds you you're alive?"

I nod. "Exactly."

She runs over another bump.

"I've already been reminded," I tell her. "Avoid the potholes."

"Sorry," she says. "I'll try."

We sail through the morning traffic, and when we get home, I've never seen anything so welcoming as our cozy Cape Cod. Even the wrap-around porch looks All-American, and I exhale as I climb out of the car.

Mila rushes ahead to unlock the door and I climb the stairs gingerly.

"Daddy, I'll read you a story," Zu offers as we walk inside. "I know two of them."

"She memorized them," Mila tells me quietly. "But that's ok. It's how I learned to read, too."

"I'd love that," I answer Zuzu. "Go get your books, sweetheart. I'll be on the couch." I head to the kitchen first to grab some icepacks, and then settle in the family room.

Surrounded by the familiar artwork and our comfortable furniture, I finally relax. Home has a way of doing that to a person.

Zuzu tucks in next to me, and 'reads' me her Dr. Suess books while Mila runs out to get my prescriptions filled, and the sweet childish voice of my daughter lulls me to sleep.

I'm awakened hours later by Mila shaking my shoulder gently, a bottle of water in her hand.

"Here," she thrusts two pills at me. "Take these."

"I'm ok," I tell her, but she's already shaking her head.

"Nope. They said to stay in front of the pain. Take them, tough guy."

"You think I'm pussy-whipped," I tell her, as I swallow the pills. "But I'm not. I'm taking these because I want to."

She laughs. "Oh, I know. It's completely your idea."

"Just so we're clear," I grumble. She laughs again.

"Your grandfather is coming over tonight to check on you."

"Really? I thought he was coming over for dinner next week."

She sighs. "Pax, you're his only grandchild. You were just hit by a car. He's coming to check on you. Also, your father called to check on you, too. You might want to call him back."

"Did you call everyone on the planet?"

She's sheepish. "I was worried. There wasn't much to do in the waiting room other than pace."

I kiss her nose, even though the movement is torture. It feels like my ribs are scraping each other, the bones digging into flesh. I ignore it.

"I love you. I'm sorry you were worried."

"I love *you* so I'll always worry. It's my job."

She bustles out, and I love watching her go, because my wife has a perfect ass. At the door, she pauses and glances back.

"I felt you staring."

I grin, and she's gone.

The pain pills make me sleepy, and so I lay my head back. The next thing I know, Mila is waking me up again. I know time has passed because shadows creep along the walls now.

"Babe, dinner is in an hour. Do you want to shower?"

I'm groggy from sleeping during the day. I'm not one for naps.

"Yeah," I mumble. "That'll be good."

Mila kisses my cheek, and her lips are warm. "Your grandfather is on his way. I've got a new bottle of Glenfiddich for him."

I shudder. "Gah. I don't know why he loves that shit."

She shrugs. "Me either. But we have a bottle for him."

My ribs feel like they are going to spring from my sternum as I get to my feet, and I imagine them tautly tuned, one by one springing free like overly tightened guitar strings. It makes me cringe, and Mila notices.

"You ok?"

"I'm perfect."

"Need more pain medicine? I think it's time."

"After I shower."

MY PEACE

She nods and I hobble down to our bathroom. It's large and from the door, it seems that the shower is a million miles away. Each step is painful, and with no one watching me, I limp pathetically. My knee is killing me, too. But I'm only a pussy if someone sees.

I let the hot water pelt my head and back, and the heat relaxes some of the pent-up tension. My bruised up body feels like it is coiled around an iron spool. I won't be hitting the gym this week, that's for sure.

Gingerly, I lather up and rinse off.

Even more gingerly, I use the towel to dry.

Lord have mercy, everything hurts. Even my scalp.

I bend slowly to dry off my feet and as I do, I glance at the wastebasket. I don't know why. My eye is just drawn to the wicker shell, and the crumpled tissues within.

There is a white plastic stick lying amid the tissue.

What the....

I reach for it, pull it out, and it is a pregnancy test.

There are two pink lines.

Chapter Four

Mila

The kitchen is warm as I bustle about. The heat makes me a bit dizzy, but I ignore it. The only side effect I get from pregnancy is sensitivity to heat.

I shove my damp hair back from my brow, and close the oven door with my foot.

"That's talent," William says from the doorway, laughing.

I glance up, and Pax's grandfather enters the room, and he seems so out of place in here in his formal suit. It doesn't matter how casual the occasion, William Alexander always wears a suit and tie, distinguished and formal.

"Not really," I tell him, smiling. "It's a necessity. With Zuzu running around, I've got to multi-task."

William smiles. "She reminds me of Pax when he was small," he says. "Except for her blonde hair, of course. She gets that from her mother."

"Yes. And my sister," I acknowledge. "But her energy… that's all Pax."

"Is there anything I can do to help?" William asks, and he leans against the granite. His hand is slender, almost skinny, with blue veins that stand out in the light.

"No, thank you," I answer. "I don't want you to get dirty."

He chuckles. "You don't think I've been inside a kitchen before."

MY PEACE

I pause. "Have you?"

He chuckles again.

"A long time ago." He looks into the distance. "But it's been years."

He seems melancholy somehow, a slight sadness perched on his mouth. William is formal, but he's always even-keeled, and never shows much emotion. He's a businessman through and through, with an amazing poker-face that has closed a thousand deals. But tonight, there's something different. Something almost sad.

"Well, you can put the rolls into a basket, if you'd like," I offer, and he actually seems relieved. He moves quickly, using tongs to pick up the browned bits of dough.

"How's Pax feeling?" he asks as he counts the rolls and arranges them.

"He's in pain," I answer. "But he's so lucky. I don't think he realizes that he could've died."

The thought almost paralyzes me. The idea that I would have to continue life without my husband. It makes my hands clammy.

William nods. "That thought crossed *my* mind when you called. I spent the entire night praying for him."

"Praying?" I lift an eyebrow. William hasn't been religious, not since Pax's mother was murdered. He always said he felt like a kind and just God wouldn't have allowed such a thing to happen. He shrugs now.

"I figured it couldn't hurt. And look... Pax is fine. So something worked."

"Yes, something did," I agree. Unconsciously, I finger my necklace. Pax had it custom made for me as a wedding gift. It's inscribed LOVE NEVER FAILS and there hasn't been a single day that has passed that I haven't worn it. It matches my mother's ring on my finger.

William looks up at me. "When are you due?"

I'm startled and my head snaps back. He laughs.

"Mila, you are the only woman I've ever met who actually glows during pregnancy. You look radiant, my dear."

I shake my head and chuckle a little.

"I just found out myself," I tell him. "I haven't even had a chance to tell Pax yet."

William smiles. "Your secret is safe with me. But I'm thrilled. Congratulations. Your little family is a source of great joy for me."

My heart warms to bursting. "Thank you."

"Hey guys," Pax greets us as he creeps into the kitchen. He moves slowly, carefully, and I know he's hurting. He's trying hard not to show it, but the man was hit by a car. Obviously, he's in pain.

Zu trails behind him.

"Grandpa!" she shrieks, and she launches herself at William. He smiles and hugs her tight, his hand in her curls.

"Zuzu-Bean," he murmurs. "Guess what I have for you?"

"Is it candy?" she asks, her eyes wide.

He nods. "Like always. But not until after dinner."

She nods happily, agreeing. "Thank you, papa."

Pax reaches out his arm and snakes it around William's shoulders, hugging him lightly.

"Good to see you, old man," he guffaws. William grins. Pax is the only one on the planet who jokes around

MY PEACE

with him in such an irreverent way, and William loves every minute of it.

"It's good to see you, son," he answers. "You hanging in there?"

"Hell, yeah," Pax answers. "It takes more than some SUV to take me down."

I shake my head and grab the bowl of vegetables. "If you guys can bring the rolls, dinner is ready."

William picks up the basket, and everyone follows me to the dining room, a room we rarely use except for when William is here. We normally gather around the kitchen table.

"Sit at the head," William instructs Pax. "This is *your* home."

Pax takes his normal seat, but he does tell William, "This is your home, too."

William smiles, and again, he seems so sad. Pax and I exchange a look, but we don't say anything. I'm not sure what to say. Perhaps William is just bothered by the accident and what 'could've been.' Lord knows, I am.

We chit-chat over dinner, about small things. Alexander Holdings, Zuzu's swimming lessons, my photography. Zuzu babbles happily, and William has seconds. He never takes his suit jacket off, but then again, I don't think I've ever seen him without it.

After dinner, he helps me clean up while Pax takes Zu upstairs.

He dries a couple of pots, then turns to me.

"Thank you for making my grandson so happy, young lady."

I'm startled by this, and I smile. "It's my pleasure. Really."

"The way you stuck by him when he was… well, let's just say when he was less than pleasant."

I have to laugh at that. When Pax's memories of what he had endured that night with his mother when she was murdered had re-emerged a few years ago, he has certainly been "less than pleasant." He had disappeared into a dark abyss and I never thought he'd come out.

But he did.

"Love never fails," I tell William simply. "Pax taught me that."

"I wish I'd been there for him," his grandfather says seriously, and now I see the source of his sadness. "All of those years."

"You and Paul had issues about Susanna. Pax knows that. We're both just glad that things are resolved now, and that everything is good," I assure him. "Pax loves you, William. Very much."

He nods. "And I love him. He's really doing amazing things at Alexander Holdings. And he's a wonderful father."

"I agree," I tell him. "He's turned out very well. You should be very proud."

"Oh, I am," he assures me. "I am."

He hugs me, and Pax hasn't come back downstairs yet.

"It's possible that he fell asleep while he was reading to Zu," I tell him. "He does that sometimes."

"It's ok. Just please thank him for me, for this evening. I'm tired, and I hear my bed calling to me."

I smile and he's gone.

I hear the front doors close, and I see the brake-lights on his car disappear into the night.

MY PEACE

I put him out of my mind as I turn off the lights, and turn on the alarm, making my way upstairs. I wake Pax, who had indeed fallen asleep in Zu's pink room. He climbs into bed with me, and we snuggle together for sleep.

I want to tell him that we're having another baby.

I'm dying to tell him.

But now is not the time. It's late, and we're tired. He's asleep within minutes, and I'm left trying to think of a really cool way to tell him. Maybe Zuzu can make him a cute video? Or I can have a custom shirt printed?

I'm still brainstorming ideas when the phone rings an hour later.

I grab at it, because it's late, and who is calling?

"Hello?" I say softly, eying Pax. It didn't wake him.

"Hello, Mrs. Tate?" It's an unfamiliar voice, although something about it seems like I've heard it before. "This is Natasha, Mr. Alexander's housekeeper."

This snaps me to attention. She's never called me before.

"Yes?"

"I'm so sorry to tell you... Mr. Alexander suffered a massive heart attack tonight. He's gone. I'm so sorry."

I'm stunned, and words won't come out, and when they do, they feel like wood.

"Gone?" My fingers are numb.

"Yes. He died immediately. It was very quick. Is Mr. Tate with you?"

"Of course. He's..." I look over. Pax's eyes are open now, wide and hazel. He stares at me, waiting. "He's right here. I'll tell him. We'll be right there."

I hang up and Pax is waiting for me to explain, and tears well up in my eyes.

He reaches for me, and he knows something terrible has happened.

"It's your grandfather…"

The words tumble out, and he sucks in a breath, but he doesn't react.

Instead, he holds me tight, strong for *me,* and strokes my hair.

"It's ok," he murmurs. "It's ok."

MY PEACE

Chapter Five

Pax

Reality stands still as my grandfather is lowered into the ground, his mahogany casket gleaming in the dying evening light.

His grave is right next to my mother's, next to her marble weeping angel and the headstone that reads *She walked in beauty, she sleeps in peace.*

My father looks up. "He's with your mother now. He's at peace." His voice is gruff.

I nod and Mila squeezes my fingers.

It's a gray, rainy day, and it is fitting for this funeral.

Well-wishers shake my head and hug Mila, and it seems like hours pass before the three of us are finally alone.

"I have your grandfather's will," my father says as we climb into the family car.

I'm startled by that, and just as startled that he would bring it up now. I wince as I click my seat-belt. The pain is still bad. After a week, I would've thought it would fade. It hasn't. In fact, the pain in my knee has gotten worse.

"I know. It's not what you want to hear today," my father adds, and the driver closes the door.

"Not really," I admit. "But why do *you* have the will?"

My father is an attorney, but not my grandfather's attorney.

"He wanted me to handle this," my dad shrugs. "Pax… William knew for some time that the end was close. He had major blockages in his heart, and they were inoperable. He wanted me to tell you directly after the funeral about the terms of his will. He wanted you to have time to think about it."

He has my attention, and I wait for him to continue. "Go on."

"I think it goes without saying that you get everything. He's got some trusts set up for charitable donations, but pretty much everything comes to you. With a couple stipulations."

"What are they?" Mila asks and her eyes are red. The past couple of days haven't been easy. She was close to William. She loved him, and he loved her. We were all he had, and she knew that. She did everything she could to make him feel included and loved.

My father clears his throat.

"You must live in his home for at least five years, and even if you choose not to continue living in it at that time, you must keep it in the family."

"Wow." That's all I can think of to say, because I don't want to live in my grandfather's home. It's too big, too sterile. Almost like a museum. But it's where my mother grew up, and because of that, my grandfather has never sold it. It's a beautiful estate, but it's just not *home.*

"And you must keep his key staff onboard for at least five years."

"Who does he consider key?" I can't help but ask, even though I'm ready to stop discussing my grandfather's affairs so soon after his burial.

"His housekeeper, Natasha. His chief business advisor, Peter. And of course, Roger."

"Five years?" Mila asks, her eyes serious. "But what if they do something egregious? Can he terminate them then?"

Dad nods. "Yeah. There's a list of terms outlined, complete with things that would be considered acceptable. They're a good staff though. He just wants to make sure they're taken care of, and have enough time to move on if they wish."

I nod. My grandfather has always been good to his employees.

"I'm sorry to bring this up right now, son," my father adds. "Truly. It was just William's wishes that you were told immediately. The size of the estate alone is staggering. You'll need to think about this."

I don't ask, and he waits, and then he sighs.

"It's worth three billion dollars, Pax."

"Holy cats," Mila sucks in her breath. "Billion with a B?"

My father nods, and I'm not surprised. My grandfather was a wizard at business.

"Ok," I say simply. "We'll discuss it. Do I have a time-limit to adhere to?"

Dad nods. "Yeah. He's given you thirty days to decide. If you decide to reject it, everything will go into a trust for Zuzu."

"So Zuzu would get saddled with those same terms?" I ask wryly. "I wouldn't do that."

"I know."

My dad stares out the window and after barren trees pass and rainy skies, he turns back to me. "Your grandfather was a good man."

"I know."

And he was. He was formal, and sometimes stern. He was dignified, but loving in his own way. Even now, he's trying to look out for me in the best ways he knows how. In trying to dictate the terms, he was trying to give himself peace of mind that I will continue making good decisions, and continue being successful in life.

I love him too much to fault him for that.

When we reach my home, my father climbs out of the car first, and then helps me out. His eagle eyes don't miss the fact that I'm moving slow, or that I flinch when the muscles in my back contract, and my knee gives a little with every step I take.

"Maybe you should go back and see your doctor?" he suggests as we head inside.

"Maybe," I acquiesce, and both he and Mila do a double-take.

"It must be bad," my wife decides. "I'll make an appointment for you for tomorrow."

I nod, and Zuzu runs into the room with Chelcie close on her heels.

"Daddy," she shrieks, and Mila catches her before she plows into me.

"Remember, daddy is fragile," Mila reminds her, and I roll my eyes.

"Again, I'll show you fragile," I remind her softly, for our ears only. Zu grabs my legs and holds on and my father pries her off, hefting her onto his back.

MY PEACE

"Show grampy your room," he tells her, galloping like a horse down the hall. Paul Tate has definitely mellowed since having a grandchild.

Mila and I stand alone in the foyer and her slender fingers find mine.

"Are you ok?" she asks softly. I think about that.

I think about how my grandfather had welcomed us into his life with open arms, and how he had insisted that I work in his family business… not because he needed someone, but because he wanted me to stay clean, and he wanted me to have something positive to focus on.

I think about the man he was, and how much he had affected me in the few years that I'd known him.

"Yeah," I say finally. "I'm happy I had a chance to know him."

Mila nods and she smiles, because she likes that answer.

"What do you think about… what your dad said?" she asks and she's hesitant. I scan her face. She's so open, so trusting. She'll do whatever I want to do. I know that.

I place my hand on her flat belly, my fingers splayed out.

"I'm not sure his home is where I want to have a baby," I tell her, and my voice is husky. Her head snaps up, her eyes meeting mine.

"How did you know?"

"You're already starting to waddle," I grin. She smacks me.

"Seriously. How did you know?"

"I saw the pregnancy test in the trash, babe."

I hug her tight, and she sighs into my arm. "Are you happy?"

"Hell, yeah," I tell her honestly. "I love putting my babies in you."

She giggles at that. "I love that process, too."

"You feeling ok?" I ask her. She was radiant with Zuzu. She was barely sick a day… until the very end, when she had almost died from a detached placenta.

"I feel great," she says brightly. "I wanted to tell you when I first found out, but then… well, I didn't want you to remember it as a sad occasion."

"I don't," I answer. "It's the circle of life. One dies, another is born. My grandpa would be happy."

Mila nods because she knows that's true. "He was happy. He guessed it that night at dinner. Said it showed on my face. He really loved us, Pax."

A knot forms in my throat. "I loved him, too."

I move, and flinch. Mila narrows her eyes at me.

"Have you taken your pain meds?"

I shake my head. "I forgot."

"You'd better do it. You've been limping all day."

Shit. I'd hoped she hadn't noticed.

"Yeah, I noticed." She raises an eyebrow.

"Do you read minds now, too?"

She grins. "Only yours."

I shake my head and limp away to the kitchen, to grab my pills. I swallow them down, and within minutes, the pain is dulled.

I'm a dumbass for forgetting.

It's not until later in the evening that I realize that when I'm medicated, I don't feel my grief as much. It's less stark, less throbbing. I guess the pain meds dull my thoughts, maybe.

I reach for the pill bottle again before bedtime.

MY PEACE

Chapter Six

"Go placidly against the noise and haste." My wife traces the words on my side, a quote from the poem *Desiderata*, as she has a hundred times before. And as she has just as many times, she utters the following sentence of the poem, even though it's not inked onto my body. "And remember what peace there is in silence."

I smile and open my eyes, the morning sunlight glinting across Mila's naked body. Even though her belly is still flat now, it will swell soon with our child. I sort of fucking love it. I palm it, my other hand stroking her back. She's perfect. Slender, graceful. Mine.

"*You're* my peace," I tell her honestly.

"I beg to differ," she arches an eyebrow. "Your name *actually means peace.* You're mine."

"Well, I'm yours and you're mine. How about that?" I offer the compromise, and she snuggles into the crook of my arm.

"Ok."

"Did you get much sleep last night?" I trail my fingers along her arm. She's sleep sensitive. If she's upset, sleep eludes her.

"Nope. But you did. You snored into my ear all night."

Even her scowl is cute.

I nip at her nose.

MY PEACE

"Sorry."

"No, you're not. But that's ok. You shouldn't have to be miserable too."

"I want to be, if you are," I tell her seriously. She grins at me.

"You've gotten kind of sickening, Pax Tate."

"I know," I agree, and I do. I'm a shell of the man I used to be, but I'm a much better man now. No one would disagree with that.

"I wanted to go to Angel Bay this week," I tell her. I'd kept my beach-house there, the loft that overlooks Lake Michigan. It's where Mila and I met. It's still our respite from the world. We retreat there whenever our schedules allow.

"Yeah, me too," she says. "But there's no way you can fly in your condition, Crash."

I roll my eyes.

"Maybe a mortal man couldn't, but you forget who you're speaking to."

She's the one rolling her eyes now.

"Uh-huh. We'll have to go later in the year. Right now, we have to think about your grandfather's will."

"Yeah." I stare out the window, at the white sky. "I don't want to live in his house," I tell her honestly. "It's not a home, it's a mausoleum. He even still has my mother's room there, preserved exactly like it was when she left for college. It freaks me out."

Mila nods. "Yeah. But hey, he didn't say we can't change the house, Pax. We can remodel. We can make it ours."

"You want to do this?" I stare at her. She shrugs.

"Babe, it's not like that's a real a question. We kind of have to. And it's only for five years. What's five years in the span of a life? Not much. And maybe we'll end up liking it."

I sigh. "I doubt it. I don't like having staff hanging around. It's weird."

She nods. "I do agree with that. But it is what it is, babe. We'll figure it out."

"You're the best wife," I announce. She nods.

"Yes. I'm glad you know it."

"I do."

"I'll call my father," I sigh as I roll out of bed. My shoulders throb and my ribs contract, but I ignore it.

"Ok. And I'll call the doctor for you," Mila says. I start to open my mouth, but she shuts me down. "No arguments."

"Fine."

I pick up the phone and call my father, and Mila disappears with her phone down the hall.

I'm in the shower when Mila comes back. "Are you having trouble breathing?" she shouts over the sound of the water. I shake my head.

"No. Only when I move."

"Ok. Then the doctor says to give it a few more days. He says that the level of pain you're having is normal for broken ribs." She turns to leave, then turns back dramatically. "Oh, by the way, you didn't tell me you have broken ribs."

I cringe. "You weren't supposed to know that part."

"Well, I do now. Get dressed, Crash. Eat breakfast, take your medicine."

She starts to leave, but I call after her. "Babe?"

MY PEACE

She pauses. "Yeah?"

"I called my father. You'd better call the movers."

Her shoulders clench for just a minute. I know how much she loves this house. But she purposely relaxes her face, and smiles.

"Great. I'll do it today."

"Great."

"Babe?" She looks at me. "Don't do too much, ok? Make sure you rest."

She pauses, then looks away. "That was a freak thing, Pax. There was something wrong with the embryo. It won't happen again."

I hate reminding her that she miscarried a couple years ago. It had devastated her, and it had crushed me. But I need her to promise that she'll take care of herself.

"I know," I assure her. "There was nothing you could've done, babe. I just want you to promise me that you're not going to overdo it now. The movers will pack. You just point at things for them."

She grimaces. "Ok."

"I know. It kills you not to be in the mix of things." I laugh and she swats at me, then remembers that I'm injured. She clasps her hand over her mouth.

"I'm sorry," she exclaims.

"You barely touched me. Don't worry about it."

But it *did* hurt. I can still feel her fingerprints on my ribcage. Jesus, I'm pathetic.

I limp into the bedroom to change my clothes, and as I do. My phone rings. The screen tells me that it's my brother-in-law.

"Hey, Gabe," I answer, trying to wiggle into a t-shirt.

"Hey, bro. How you feeling?"

As if I'm going to tell the big ex-Ranger the truth, that I'm sore as hell.

"I'll make it," I tell him.

"Good. Maddy wants me to take you out tonight so that she can hang with the girls… do manicures and shit, I guess."

I know Mila would like it. I know she surely can't wait to tell Maddy the baby news.

"Ok," I agree. "What do you have in mind?"

"How about the Crow's Nest? Seven o'clock?"

"I'll be there."

My body screams at me, and I decide I'd better take a fucking nap to rest up. I medicate myself first, then sleep for three peaceful hours.

***

"Don't do it," Gabe warns, his dark eyebrow raised. I examine the full shot glass of whiskey in front of me. "You haven't had anything to drink in forever. Plus, you're on pain meds. You're gonna regret it in the morning."

He's probably right, but I'm sure as hell not going to admit it.

"I am not one to shirk from a challenge," I announce, and the room is only slightly wobbly. My leg slips off the bar-stool and I put it back, hoping Gabe doesn't notice.

He does.

And he smirks.

"Whatever, Tate," he drawls, knocking back his own shot. "It's eight to eight. Are we going to make it to ten?"

MY PEACE

"What are we celebrating, again?" I ask, shooting the tequila, then wiping my mouth. The bitter taste slides down my throat, and it's almost foreign. I don't drink much nowadays.

Gabe grins. "Your upcoming new baby."

"Oh, yeah," I pretend to remember. "My baby."

He rolls his eyes.

"Mila is going to kill me for bringing you home drunk," he says. "I can't remember the last time we did this."

"It's been too long," I agree. "It's good. We needed it." Plus, being drunk, it makes my body hurt less. I can barely feel it right now. That's got to be a plus.

Gabe is hesitant though, and glances at my empty glass. "You good, though?"

I know what he is asking. A few years ago, I slid deep into the hole of using alcohol and drugs as a way of dealing with life. But I'm not in that place now. I dealt with my shit, and while I don't usually drink anymore, I'm ok to celebrate once in a while.

"I'm good," I assure him. "Trust me."

"Okay." His answer is simple and immediate. He and I hadn't gotten off on the best of terms when he started dating my wife's sister, mainly because Gabe had his own demons to fight. But he'd fought them and won, and he's as good a man as I've ever known.

"Pool?" I gesture toward the empty table, and we slide off our barstools.

Gabe cocks an eyebrow. "You up for that, dude?" He's doubtful, and I know if I were sober, it would hurt too damn much to play. But I'm not sober.

"Bite me."

"Twenty bucks?" Gabe glances at me, his giant bicep flexing as he moves. I'm pretty sure he's trying to intimidate me.

"Sure." We grab sticks and chalk, and Gabe racks the balls. "And winner buys the next round."

"I hope you brought your wallet."

We chuckle together and I break, and the game is on.

He goes, then I go, and we're neck in neck.

"You summa bitch," Gabe mutters as I knock another into the back pocket. I laugh.

"You should know by now never to challenge me, dude."

He rolls his eyes. "Whatever. I shit bigger than you."

"Charming."

I'm thinking of something else to say when a disturbance catches my eye.

In the back, next to the bathroom hallway, a man and a woman argue. It's heated and they are both pissed. She waves her arms in the air, and he grabs her wrist.

I pause. Gabe pauses.

The guy gets into her face, and then shoves her against the wall.

Gabe and I move at the same time, dropping our sticks on the pool table.

Striding across the room, we are step-in-step with each other. Gabe deftly grabs the guy from behind and hauls him away from the girl.

I step in his face.

"Pick on someone your own size," I tell him firmly.

He scowls, and he's got a scar on earlobe. "This isn't your business." He wrenches away from Gabe. "Get off me."

MY PEACE

He backs up a step, but Gabe is a solid wall and catches him. He struggles, and his girlfriend pleads with him.

"Seth, just stop. Let's go."

I glance at her. "I wouldn't suggest going anywhere with him."

But she glares at me, and grabs his arm.

"You should mind your own business."

They stalk away, and Seth sends me a death stare over his shoulder as they go.

"That's fucked up, dude," Gabe says as we watch them walk out the door.

"You can't save some people," I agree. "She'll have to decide when she's ready to stop being abused."

Gabe shakes his head, and we finish our game. When I knock the eight-ball into the back pocket at the end, he rolls his eyes, and holds out a twenty.

"I always pay up."

I grin and snatch it up. "And you owe this round."

"Rub it in," he mutters as he heads to the bar. He comes back a few minutes later with our last shots.

"This makes ten," he announces. "We're going to feel this tomorrow."

We slam the shots, thunking our glasses on the table at the same time.

I squint my eyes as I swallow, then shake my head, like I'm shaking the bad taste away.

"Damn," I mutter. "This is gonna leave a mark."

My head feels thick and heavy, and I remember why I laid off drinking. I don't much like the numbing effect. Not anymore.

"We'd better not drive," Gabe says wisely. I agree.

"Yeah."

"You call Mila," he suggests.

I scoff. "Fuck that. You call Maddy."

"Hell no, she'll kick my ass."

"Well, Mila will kick mine," I answer. "Besides, Zu's already in bed asleep. Mila can't leave."

"Well, Eli's sleeping too," Gabe replies. "And the baby. Maddy can't come."

"We're both p-whipped and scared of our wives," I point out.

"No, we're smart," Gabe argues. "I'll call Brand."

He pulls out his phone, dials, and soon, he's talking to Brand Killien, his boyhood best friend and brother-in-law.

"I know it's late," he sighs. "I'm sorry, dude. Please tell Nora we're sorry for bothering you guys."

He hangs up. "He'll be here in twenty."

I nod, because I knew he would, because Brand is the kind of guy is always there when you need him. He always has been, and always will be. Gabe served with him in the Army and they are both decorated soldiers.

They don't leave another in the field, even if tonight, the 'field' is a dive bar.

We wait out in the cool air, breathing deeply, as we wait for Brand to arrive. Soon enough, his big pick-up pulls in the lot, and his eyes are red.

"You guys look like shit," he says sleepily, and his blond hair is mussed.

"Gabe tried to kill me," I tell him as I climb into the front seat. Gabe guffaws from the back.

"Whatever, Tate. It was your idea."

MY PEACE

"You're both dumbasses," Brand decides as he pulls out of the parking lot. "And may God have mercy on your souls when your wives see you."

That honestly shuts us both up. Mila will kill me... mainly because I skipped my evening dose of pain meds just so I could have a drink with Gabe.

The truck is quiet, and then after a while, Brand speaks.

"I'm so sorry about your grandfather, dude. Is there anything I can do?"

"Thank you," I answer, my forehead resting on the cool window. God, the cold feels good on my face. "No, there's nothing anyone can do. But thank you for offering."

"Anytime," he answers. "Anything. You know that."

"I do," I agree. "You're a good man, Brand."

I don't hear his reply because I pass out slumped against the door. The next thing I know, Brand is carefully hefting me out of the truck.

"Careful with his ribs," Gabe calls from the backseat. He's splayed on the seat, his arm thrown over his eyes. It gives me satisfaction to know that he's not in any better condition than I am.

"I can't feel them right now," I assure Brand.

"I bet you can't," he grins. He walks with me to the back door. "You good from here?"

"Of coursh," I slur. He cocks an eyebrow. I try again. "Of coursh."

He shakes his head. "Night, dude. Sleep it off."

I creep through the house, but I realize I'm not creeping when I slam my foot into an ottoman in the living room.

"Summabitch," I curse at it.

"Pax?" Mila stands in the doorway in one of my t-shirts. "Are you ok?"

"Yeah, babe," I assure her. "I'm sorry to wake you up."

She eyes me. "Oh lord. You and Gabe did a number on yourselves."

I start to apologize, but she holds up a hand. "Lord knows, you needed to blow off some steam. Let's get you to bed. Do you feel like throwing up yet?"

I shake my head. "Nah. I don't throw up."

I am, of course, vomiting within the hour. I make it to the bedroom, and I retch into the toilet, and by now, I can feel my ribs again. The pain is excruciating every time I heave.

"Fuck." I wipe off my mouth, then brush my teeth before I head back to bed.

Something bothers me, but I can't put my finger on it. Something, something niggles at me. But I put it out of my mind and fall back to sleep.

Whiskey makes sleep restless, though. I wake again a few hours later, when it is still dark outside.

There's a gnawing feeling in my gut and I think on it for a minute.

It's familiar, and my mind is fuzzy.

I wake up enough to focus.

It's a hunger, but I'm not hungry.

There's an ache in my body, a need for something, something black, something hateful. In my sleep, I had tasted it in my mouth, the bitterness of cocaine, the sweetness of heroine, and I swallow hard. My hand shakes, and I swear to God it's on my tongue, smeared on my teeth, causing my heart to pound out of my chest.

MY PEACE

Only it's not.

It was a dream.

For the first time in years, I'm dreaming about drugs. *Son of a bitch.*

The knowledge slams into me, hard and fast.

I sit up and grab my water glass from the nightstand, gulping the fresh liquid down, trying to drown out the remnants of a taste I haven't had in so long.

What the fuck is wrong with me?

Why would I be craving that shit now?

"Pax?"

Mila's voice is small and clear in the dark, like a bell, and she reaches for me. "You ok?"

"Yeah, babe," I lie. I can't tell her what I'm craving. She'd be devastated and worried, and she doesn't need that. It's the first secret I've kept from her. It's not something I take lightly.

"Hold me." Mila snuggles up against me, her body slight and soft. Her arm reaches around and pulls me back, into the bed, next to her.

Her warmth, her smell... it's familiar. It's mine.

This is where I belong.

Not in the oblivion I once craved.

I close my eyes, and the blackness is there, behind my eyelids, and once upon a time, I would have disappeared in it gladly. Tonight, though, I think about my wife. I think about my daughter. I think about the life in Mila's belly. I think of sunshine. I don't know when I finally fall back to sleep.

All I know is that I do.

Chapter Seven
Mila

The Mansion, as Pax and I call it, is flooded with movers.

"Where would you like this, m'am?" one asks me. He's holding a box clearly marked "Nightstand."

"In the master bedroom," I tell him patiently. I start to pick up a box, but Pax is walking through the door and he eyes me. I stand back up, my hands empty.

"I can't believe they were able to renovate the master in just a month," I say to divert his attention. "It's incredible."

"Well, it was my grandfather's for fifty years. It needed a facelift," he answers. He pulls me to him. "I paid them extra to have it done in time for you."

I kiss him softly.

"We're going to be ok here," I assure him. "I don't want you to worry. Wherever you are, it's home."

"You're just trying to distract me from lecturing you about resting," he tells me.

"I hate that you know me so well."

He chuckles. "Ha. Get used to it."

"Are you going to work?"

He nods. He'd been off for a couple of weeks to recover, but now that he's healing up, he's back in the swing of things. "Yeah. Roger's probably waiting outside right now."

"Ok. Have a great day. Hopefully a lot will be done by the time you get home."

"Not by you though," he says sternly.

"Ok. Not by me."

He's out the door before I know it, and I'm alone again with the movers. Maddy took Zuzu for a playdate with Eli, so I can actually rest for a minute.

I drop into a chair in the formal living room, and put my feet up on the gleaming coffee table in front of me.

"M'am, that is an antique," a voice says to me.

I turn my head to find the housekeeper, Natasha, in the doorway. She's troubled, I can tell, by my disregard for the formal furniture.

"I know," I tell her gently. "But my home is to be lived in, not looked at."

She moves across the room, and I find myself wondering, once again, why such a young woman would want to be a housekeeper for an elderly man like William. She's around thirty, slender, pretty with long caramel hair that she keeps twisted into a bun.

"Would you like some chamomile tea?" she asks. "You seem stressed."

"I *am* stressed," I admit. "Moving does that to a person."

Natasha nods sympathetically. "Mr. Tate instructed me to watch out for you."

"You mean, supervise me?" I ask dubiously. She smiles, and she has a nice smile. It seems sincere.

"Maybe," she admits. "He doesn't want you to overdo it."

"I'm only eleven weeks pregnant," I tell her. "I'm fine. But if he asks, tell him I rested all day."

"Should I make you some breakfast?" she asks. "I can bring you some eggs and fruit, if you like?"

"That would be lovely," I answer. "Thank you."

I agree with Pax. I don't like having people hovering about, but having someone cook me breakfast doesn't suck. Natasha disappears into the massive house and I close my eyes. The first trimester is exhausting.

Last time, I'd miscarried at thirteen weeks.

I have it in my head that if I can just get past that milestone, all will be well this time. It's probably not rational, but it's how I think.

A mover pops his head in. "Miss? I have art supplies. Where should I put them?"

"The loft above the garage," I tell him. Pax is turning it into a studio for me, only it's not finished yet. It will overlook the pond behind the house, which should be relaxing.

Hey, you resting? Pax texts me.

I shake my head. *Yes. And thank you for putting a spy on my tail.*

Hahaha. I have to keep you in line somehow.

Whatever.

I'll bring you home a burrito from El Loco's.

I love you, I answer immediately.

I know the way to a preggo's heart.

I smile. I'm so lucky.

Even now, as I look around the giant formal room with cathedral ceilings and wooden walls, I know that even though I don't love this house, the opportunities available to us are such a blessing.

I can make this house my own, I decide, as Natasha comes back in with a tray.

"I'm going to be making a few changes," I tell her as she arranges it on the side-table.

"Oh?" she asks casually.

"Yes. I want to make it homier here. So we feel more... well, at home."

"That's understandable," she answers. "Where would you like to start?"

"Well, I'll have the designer who is doing my studio come talk to me about it."

Natasha nods. "Would you like anything else?"

I shake my head. "This is perfect. Thank you."

"I'll be back for your tray a bit later," she tells me before she leaves again.

I sigh as a I take a bite of juicy melon. No, having Natasha here doesn't suck.

When she leaves, I realize that I don't even know if she lives here, or off the premises. This house is really that big.

I sigh, as I think about everything I'll have to learn.

It's ok, though.

This is a blessing, I remind myself. *A blessing.*

So is the baby in my belly.

I lay my hand on my abdomen, and imagine the life that lives within. Will it be a boy who looks like Pax? Or a girl who looks like me? I don't want to tell Zuzu until I'm further along. Not with my track record.

But Maddy though... I can tell my sister.

And I do... when she brings Zuzu home later in the day.

Eli and Zu are running through the empty corridors, and Maddy sits next to me on the couch.

"Spill it," she says, examining me. "You want to tell me something."

I stare at her, dumbfounded. "How do you always know?"

She laughs, pushing her blond hair back with a manicured hand. "I know you, Mi. You know that."

I take a breath.

"Ok. Well, I'm pregnant."

Maddy stares at me for a second before she shrieks and launches herself at me, wrapping herself around my neck. Her grip is like a vise, and it's actually hard to breathe.

"Should I call for security, m'am?" Natasha says wryly as she comes in to get my tray. I grimace.

"Maybe."

Maddy swats at me. "Bite your tongue. When are you due?"

"I'm eleven weeks," I answer. "So I'm being cautious. Don't tell anyone, Mad. I mean it. You know what happened last time."

She grabs my hand. "You know that miscarriages happen, sweetie. It will be ok this time. I feel it. Pax knows, right?"

I nod. "Of course. And Natasha, and William knew before he passed. That's it."

"Do you need anything else, Mrs. Tate?" Natasha waits. I shake my head.

"No, thank you." She turns, and I speak again. "Wait. Do you live here?"

She twists back around. "M'am?"

I feel silly. "I mean, do you live in this house?"

She smiles. "Yes. I have a room off of the kitchen."

She disappears, and Maddy turns to me. "Do you really have security?"

MY PEACE

I laugh, and lift my tea cup. "No." I take a drink. "I don't think so anyway."

She rolls her eyes, and it's just her and me… me and my sister, and this giant house suddenly doesn't seem so bad. I can hear the kids' laughter echoing from somewhere down the hall, playing hide and seek, and it's all going to be ok.

I feel it.

Maddy visits for over an hour, only leaving when the baby starts to get cranky. It doesn't escape my attention that she doesn't leave until it's almost time for Pax to be home. They're clearly taking turns sitting with me.

I freshen up, and and am waiting for my husband when he comes through the door.

"Hey, babe, he greets me. His suit fits him perfectly, although he has loosened his tie. I'm pretty sure it's the first thing he does when he walks out the office door. "How was your day? Did you rest?"

"Yep," I tell him honestly. "Maddy visited, the kids played. It was good."

"Good," he answers, and pulls me to him. "Gimme some of that."

I smile against his lips, and he kisses me hard. "I missed you today," he admits, and he grips my butt in one hand.

"Good," I grin.

"Is it bedtime yet?" he growls into my neck. I smile. "Not yet."

He releases me. "Fine. Play hard to get. You'll get yours."

I laugh, and we play with Zu for a while after Pax changes clothes. Honestly, I like him better in jeans and a t-shirt. A suit just isn't him, even if he *does* wears it well.

At dinner time, we sit in the dining room, and the table is so long. There is room for twenty at it, and the wood gleams in the candle-light.

Zuzu stares at me from across the table.

"Mama, our new house is big."

Pax chuckles at her troubled expression. "Is that a problem, Zu?"

She shakes her head. "No, daddy. I just… I just… can I have a puppy now?"

"You little opportunist," Pax smiles. "We'll see."

"You shouldn't be too surprised," I tell him. "She's your daughter, through and through."

He grins at me over his water glass.

After dinner, we have our dessert in the main family room. Natasha seems troubled as she brings us the tray with three pie plates.

"Mr. Alexander never ate in here," she tells us. "This rug was shipped from Turkey. It's very expensive."

Pax's head snaps up, and he takes a plate from her.

"Natasha, I assume you know about Mr. Alexander's will… how we have to employ you for five years?"

Natasha stands up straight. "Yes, sir."

"That doesn't entail you telling me or my wife what to do. That isn't in your job description. I don't know how your relationship with my grandfather went, but our relationship with you will not be that way."

Natasha looks sheepish, and I almost feel sorry for her, even though her attitude all day has been annoying.

MY PEACE

"This is our home now," Pax continues. "We will treat it as a home, not a museum. I'll thank you to not make us feel uncomfortable about that."

Natasha nods reluctantly. "Yes, sir."

She starts to leave.

"You will be employed here for five years," Pax tells her. "But we aren't required to keep you in your current position."

Natasha freezes, her shoulders tight. She turns. "Sir?"

"You are the housekeeper. You do not tell my wife and I how to live. If you do, we'll find another position for you."

"Yes, sir. I'm sorry."

Pax relaxes. "I don't mean to sound harsh, Natasha. But my first priority is my wife. I don't want her to feel uncomfortable here. She's given up a lot to be with me."

I startle. "Pax," I start to say. He glances at me.

"You have," he tells me. "You didn't want to come here. I know that. But you did it because you love me. This is your home. Do what you want with it. If you want to burn every damn piece of furniture in it and start over, you can."

Natasha gasps and I rush to reassure her.

"I'm not burning things, Natasha. In fact, if I decide I don't want something, I'll offer it to you."

She exhales. "Thank you, m'am, although you don't have to do that."

"You care about this house," I point out. "That's commendable. Thank you."

She nods and she's gone and I stare at my husband.

"Holy shit, Pax."

He shrugs. "It needed to be said."

I shake my head and snuggle into my husband's shoulder. "I love you."

He glances down at me. "I know."

We watch Zuzu inhale her pie and dance around the room, spinning and twirling, because it's as big as a gymnasium.

"Should I put her to bed?" Pax asks me. "It's getting late."

He's hopeful, and I know why. I grin.

"Yeah. Let's do it on our way to bed."

She does down surprisingly fast, and snuggles into her bed. Hers was the first room I had repainted. It is a pale blue in here now, her favorite color and it's very soothing. Tomorrow, I'm painting ivy vines twisting around her walls. I want to turn it into a "secret garden" themed room. She'll love it.

Our master suite is right down the hall, through a set of double doors.

It was recently stripped of wall-paper and repainted bone-white. It's got airy curtains, floor to ceiling, and we have a new bed. It's a massive wooden piece and it faces a large fireplace.

Classic, slightly masculine. I want Pax to be able to unwind in here.

After we brush our teeth and settle into bed, I cuddle against my husband.

"I love that you still sleep naked," he murmurs into my ear. He runs his large hand over my hip, up my ribcage. His fingers are careful, like I'm made of glass.

"Lord, I want to be in you," he says, his voice husky.

I turn, pressing into him. "So be in me."

MY PEACE

He groans. "No. I want to wait. Until after the first trimester."

I startle, even though that's only a week away.

"You think you'll hurt me?"

"I don't want to take any chances," he says and he's almost sheepish. "I want you, Mi. Don't doubt that."

He's rock hard against my leg, so I don't question his desire.

"Fine," I say finally. "You don't have to be in me. However… you can't tell me what to do, so…."

I climb up and over him, kneeling, and take him in my mouth.

"Son of a bitch," he bleats, and he tries to pull me off. "That's not fair to you, Mi. You don't have to."

I pause. "I want to. I love you, Pax."

I slide him in and out, my fingers around his balls, clenching softly, then with more pressure. My husband's breathing hitches, and hitches.

"Jesus," he finally manages to say, and his grasp is tight on my ass. "I'm gonna cum, babe."

He pulls away from me and comes on his own belly, and his head drops back on the pillow.

"You're going to be the death of me," he says weakly.

I grin.

"There's no better way to go," I offer.

He grins, his eyes still closed. "True."

He cleans up with a tissue, and we settle in for sleep. He drifts off within minutes, but I'm awake a long time.

This house is old, and the noises it makes are new to me. It will take me a while to get used to them, to know what is normal and what is not.

I lay my hand on my belly. In a couple of weeks, I should be able to feel the baby move. I smile at that, and I'm almost... almost... asleep when Pax moans next to me.

He writhes and turns and moans, and then finally, he wakes up with a loud yelp, sitting straight up in bed.

"Babe?" I ask, stroking his back. "You're ok. You're ok. Was it a nightmare?"

He's rubbing his knee absently and he nods. "Yeah. I guess it was."

"Does your knee hurt?" He's been limping from time to time, and it's worried me.

"A little. It's nothing to worry about."

I do worry though, and he knows it. He opens his arms to me, and I settle in against him, listening to his strong heart beat until I finally fall asleep.

MY PEACE

Chapter Eight

Pax

Sweet Jesus, the pain.

My knee sends spirals of vise-like pain up into my leg, and it's enough to take my breath away.

I'd gone to the doctor today, and heard the verdict. I need knee-surgery. The ligaments and tendons around my knee were torn badly in the accident, frayed beyond the ability to mend themselves. But I'm not putting Mila through the stress of that. Not until after she's past the point of possible miscarriage.

I'll deal with the pain for a couple more weeks. I'm no pussy.

I lay still until her breathing is deep and even, and she begins snoring in her cute little snorts. I smile in the dark, and then carefully, carefully, ease out of her embrace. She stirs a little, and I freeze on the edge of the bed. She settles back in without waking up. In her sleep, she reaches out for me, and I push my pillow toward her. She grabs it and pulls it to her chest. I smile and slip out of the room.

I feel like a wounded soldier as I limp down the long hall toward my study and switch on a lamp.

Once my grandfather's, it is a huge room with a massive fireplace and wood-paneled walls. It's a gentleman's room, and the irony as I sit behind the desk is not lost on me.

I'm no gentleman. At least, not the kind this room was intended for.

This room was built back when men retired after dinner with scotch and cigars while the women huddled together and did cross-stich.

That's so not Mila and me.

I stretch my leg out and rub at the knee.

Rubbing it doesn't help much, but it makes me think I'm doing something for it.

"Mr. Tate?"

I look up to find Natasha in the doorway, clad in a floor-length robe.

"Is everything ok? I saw your light."

Her hair is down now, and it makes her seem less stern, more her age.

"Everything is fine," I assure her. "I couldn't sleep."

She glances at my hand rubbing my knee. "Can I get your pain pills for you?"

I've been trying not to take them, but Lord. Pain is pain.

"Ok. Thank you."

She disappears, and comes back in a few minutes with a glass of water and two pills.

She pours them into my hand and watches me as I knock them back.

"Acknowledging pain isn't a weakness," she tells me quietly.

"I know that," I say, more sharply than I intended. "Sorry."

"Do you, though?" she wonders. "Because I see you trying to hide it."

"My wife has enough to worry about," I say stiffly. "She doesn't need to worry about this, too."

MY PEACE

Natasha stares at me doubtfully. "I'm pretty sure she'd want to know."

I *know* she would. But it's not what is best for her. Not yet.

"You don't understand," I say, and I don't know why I'm explaining. "Mila had a miscarriage last time. I just want to keep her stress-free for the next couple of weeks until she's out of the danger. Most people miscarry in the first twelve weeks, if they're going to miscarry."

"You're sweet to worry," Natasha says finally. "I'll help you however you want me to help."

I didn't ask her to help.

"If you can just make sure she rests," I tell her. "When I'm at work. She has a tendency to do too much."

Natasha nods. "Of course."

"Thank you."

"Anything else?"

I shake my head. "No, thank you."

"Very well. I'll keep this between us."

I didn't ask her to.

"As you wish."

She nods and she's gone.

I'm alone again in my study, and the pain pills have begun to kick in. They're taking the edge off, at least. I can breathe around the pain now.

I answer a couple of e-mails, waiting to see if I get even more relief as time passes. I don't.

With a sigh, I eye my grandfather's bar on the other side of the room. A throw-back to times lost, it's a full-bar.

Without giving myself a moment to second-guess, I cross the room, pour a couple fingers of scotch, and gulp it down.

That should help.

And it does. Within minutes, the pain has dulled. Hopefully, enough to sleep. I make my way quietly back to my bedroom, slip in next to Mila, and drift off to sleep.

***

"Mr. Tate, your two o'clock is here."

Sasha's voice is loud on my phone's intercom. It snaps me awake, because I'd almost dozed off. Sleeping only a couple of hours because of pain sucks balls.

"Thank you, Sasha," I answer, punching at the button. "Send them in."

I don't even know who my two o'clock is. That's how dim-witted I feel today. I rub at my eyes, and then rub at my knee.

I'm a fucking mess.

"Dude, you look like shit."

Gabe strides in, with Brand on his heels. They are both dressed in slacks and button-up shirts.

"You're my two o'clock?" I roll my eyes and stand up. "I thought it was a real meeting."

Gabe stares at me indignantly. "We *are* a real meeting. We have fourth quarter profit and loss statements to go over with you."

"Snore," I tell him.

"Why do you look like shit?" Brand asks me curiously, as he sets his briefcase down on my conference table in the corner.

"I didn't realize that I do."

"You do," he assures me.

MY PEACE

"You still hurtin'?" Gabe asks, his brow furrowed. "I've got the name of a damn good PT if you want it. He can get you straightened out."

I sigh. "I apparently need surgery on my knee. I blew it out. But I don't want to for a couple of weeks. I don't want to upset Mila."

Gabe lifts an eyebrow. "Mila is the most unflappable person I know."

"She's pregnant," I tell them. "I don't want to stress her out."

"Dude," Brand exclaims. "Congratulations!" They both slap me on the back, and I cringe because that pain ricochets down into my hips, straight into my knee. I grit my teeth and hide it though. Damned if I'll show my pain to these two.

"Thanks," I say instead.

"Ok. Well, how about this. We made money in the fourth quarter," Gabe says. "A lot of it. We can send the specifics to Peter, if you want. But tonight, let's go celebrate. Cancel your afternoon."

Peter is the business advisor I inherited from my grandfather. I'll gladly relegate paperwork to him.

I eye my calendar. There's nothing on it for the rest of the day.

"Fine," I tell them. "I've got til five o'clock."

"That's all we need," Brand tells me.

We walk out of my office, and Sasha scrambles up. "I'll have your car waiting for you," she calls after me.

Gabe stops in his tracks. "Your car? As in, a car that you don't drive yourself?"

"No need," I tell Sasha. "I'll ride with these yay-whos."

They continue to rib me all the way to Brand's truck.

"Seriously. You're too important to drive now?" Gabe asks as we climb in. "You've gotta be kidding, bro."

"I love to drive," I argue, and I wistfully think of my beloved '69 Charger sitting in my garage at home, covered with a tarp. "My grandfather just liked the idea of being driven. He thought it was a good image for the employees to see."

"Well, guess what?" Gabe tells me as Brand fires up his truck. "You're the boss now."

"That's very true." I don't tell them that at the moment, I don't think my right knee would be able to take the workings of the pedals.

I start to text Mila, to let her know I'll be out of the office for a few hours, but my phone is dead.

"Shit. I really have to be home on time."

Gabe rolls his eyes. "Dude, we're having a drink. Not kidnapping you to Tijuana."

I know I should just go home. But the idea of dulling the pain a little is appealing. And seriously... what could happen? I'm with Gabe and Brand. I don't know why I'm hesitant.

When I climb out of the truck at the pub, my knee almost gives out. Brand grabs my arm, catching me from collapsing onto the pavement.

"Dude, this isn't good." He's concerned. "I don't think you should be bearing weight on that."

I shouldn't be. The doctor told me as much.

"I'll be fine," I assure him.

After I limp inside and get situated in a booth, I prop my foot on a nearby chair. I don't intend on leaving this spot.

MY PEACE

I signal for the waitress, and order a whiskey. Gabe and Brand get one too, and when the girl is gone, Gabe glances at me.

"You know, I guess I should've asked… is this ok? You haven't been out drinking in a long time. I don't want it to cause you a problem. You know, after…"

"After what?" I stare him in the eyes and make him say it.

"After a few years ago. When you had… your issues."

"My issues were never being an alcoholic," I remind him. "Did I use it to lose myself? Yeah, I guess I did. But that was a choice I made. When you're an alcoholic, it's a need. I didn't *need* to. I *wanted* to. I'm fine."

He doesn't look completely convinced, but doesn't say anything more.

Our drinks are delivered, and I drink mine quickly.

Within a minute, my chest is warm, and within another five, the pain has dulled. I signal for another. If one is good, two is better.

Chapter Nine

Mila

There is something wet between my legs.

I realize that as I watch Zuzu play in the back gardens, and I am sitting in the shade of the house, curled up a chair.

I'm bleeding.

I call for Natasha. She comes out, casually at first, then she sees my face.

"What's wrong?" she asks in alarm.

"I need to go to the doctor, I tell her. "Please watch Zuzu."

I am out the door, leaving her staring after me in confusion.

I try to call Pax from the car, but his phone goes straight to voicemail. I call his office.

"I'm sorry, Mrs. Tate," Sasha tells me. "He left for the day over an hour ago."

"Are you sure?" I ask her. Because he hasn't come home.

"Quite sure," she assures me.

"Ok," I answer, hanging up. I call Maddy next.

"I'll meet you at the hospital," she responds, after I explain.

She actually beats me there, and when I arrive, she is pacing in front of the ER doors.

"Where's Pax?" she asks, glancing around me.

"I don't know."

We head to the admittance desk, and within thirty minutes, I'm in an exam room, with my gown tied in the back.

"If you could like flat," the doctor tells me, "We'll have a look-see."

He's got a sonogram wand in his hand, and the gel is warm on my belly. I hold my breath as he searches for a heartbeat and Maddy clutches my hand.

Then,

Then,

There it is.

A strong whirring noise, fast and loud, like a hummingbird's wings.

"There it is," the doctor says triumphantly. "It sounds good."

He pushes and prods, and examines the sonogram screen.

"I don't see any visible signs of distress," he tells me. "Sometimes, vaginal bleeding can occur for unexplained reasons. Let's put you on bed-rest this week, and you can follow up with your doctor on Monday."

I nod, and I'm so relieved. Maddy hugs me.

"It's ok," she tells me. "It's ok."

I feel weak and relieved, and Maddy slips out so I can wipe the goop off and get dressed. I try to call Pax again.

No answer.

What the hell?

I feel shaky with my relief, and Maddy wants to drive me home.

I shake my head. "No. Then we'll just have to come back for my car. It's easier this way."

Maddy stares at me. "You can send someone for your car. You have that luxury now."

I forgot. "You're right."

I leave my car and climb into Maddy's. She makes only one stop, and that is in the drive-through of a hamburger joint to get food and milkshakes.

"You have to keep your strength up," she justifies, as she shoves fries in her mouth.

"What about you?"

"Sister solidarity."

"Valid," I nod, sipping on my chocolate shake. I keep one hand on my belly protectively, as though it will help.

"You're ok," Maddy reminds me at a stoplight. "All is well."

I nod. "Ok."

"Quit worrying. That only makes things worse."

She calls Gabe through her Bluetooth.

"Hey, babe!" he answers on the speaker, and it's loud in the background. "What's up?"

"I'm just driving Mila home from the hospital," she tells him. "I might be a little late coming home."

"The hospital?" Gabe is surprised, and I hear him talking in the background with someone. Then Pax is on the phone.

"Maddy, why was Mila in the hospital? Is she all right?"

The sound of his familiar voice makes me relax into the seat, immediately comfortable.

My Pax.

"I'm fine, babe," I tell him. "Just a little blood. I freaked out and went to the ER. I couldn't get ahold of you…"

MY PEACE

"My damned phone was dead," he tells me quickly. "Gabe and Brand took me for a drink, and I planned to be home on time. I still will be. In fact, we'll leave right now. I'll meet you at home."

"You're at a bar?" I ask him, confused. This isn't like him.

"Yeah. It's no big deal, babe. I'm so sorry you couldn't reach me. That will never happen again. My phone will always be charged."

"Ok," I answer, but I'm still a bit bewildered. Pax hasn't touched much alcohol at all in years. I'm not concerned, just… startled, I guess. This is twice in a week.

Maybe he's decided, after all this time, that he's ok with it.

That's probably a good sign. Maybe? I don't know.

"Mila, I love you," he tells me. "I'll see you soon."

He hangs up, and Maddy looks at me. "See? He's fine. You're fine. All is well."

She drives for a minute or two longer, then gives me side-eye.

"Should he be at a bar?"

"Pax knows his limitations," I say firmly, and I believe that. "He chose to give up alcohol. If he thinks he can handle it now, then he can. I trust him."

"Of course!" Maddy answers. "I trust him too."

But we're quiet, and I think we're both wondering the same thing. Does Pax know what is best?

"His grandfather *did* just die," Maddy says a bit later. "And you've had to move. And his leg is hurting him. I can tell. That's a lot of change. And he's worried about you, too."

"I know," I tell her. "Trust me. But Pax would say something if he felt overwhelmed. He doesn't keep things from me. Not anymore."

"That's true," Maddy admits, and she sounds relieved. "That's very true."

"So stop worrying," I tell her. "All is well."

"Don't use my own words against me," she demands indignantly. "That's a very wise line, and I'm the one who uses it."

I roll my eyes. "Ok. You own the line."

"Damn straight."

I nibble at my hamburger for the rest of the trip, and when we get to my home, Maddy shuffles me out and into the house. She hovers like a mother hen, and makes sure I go straight to the couch.

"You're supposed to be on bed-rest this week," she reminds me. "No walking around. Just to the bathroom."

"Yes, mother."

She glares. "Don't take this lightly."

I roll my eyes again. "Do you really think I'll take it lightly?"

"No. I suppose not."

She's in the kitchen getting me a drink of water when Pax rushes through the door. He's limping, of course, but he's moving fast. Gabe and Brand are on his heels.

"Are you ok?" he asks, and he sits next to me, shoving my hair out of my eye. "Are you ok?"

"Yes," I assure him. "I'm fine. I swear to God."

He swallows. "And the baby is…"

"Okay, too. I'm supposed to be on bed-rest this week, and then follow up with Dr. Sturgeon on Monday. It's ok. All is well."

MY PEACE

Maddy clears her throat as she comes back in, and I stare at her. "It is," I insist.

"I know," she says, setting my tray down. "I coined the phrase."

"You did not," Gabe guffaws. "Brand taught you that."

"Oh, did he?" I ask, my eyebrows raised, and Maddy has the grace to look sheepish. Brand grins.

"It's something my grandma used to say," he tells us. "Are you feeling ok, Mila?"

I nod. "Yeah. Thank you for bringing Pax." I turn to my husband. "My car is at the hospital. We'll have to go get it."

"Don't worry about it," he reassures me. "It'll be taken care of."

Maddy covers my legs with a blanket. "Are you ok now? Do you need anything else?"

"If she does, I'll get it for her," Pax tells her. "Don't worry, Mad."

"As if," I say under my breath, and Gabe hears. He grins.

"You know her too well. You'd better silence your phone tonight. She might try to call you at midnight to check on you."

"Good idea."

"Very funny," Maddy announces. "You guys think you know me so well."

"We do," Gabe tells her. "Now let's go and let your sister rest."

She kisses me. "If you need anything, you call me. I mean it."

"Thanks, Mad."

They leave, and Brand goes with them. Pax and I are left alone.

"What's happening?" I ask him quietly. "Why do I feel so nervous?"

But Pax holds my hand and everything is fine, because it always is when he's with me.

"All is well," he says, and he smiles and it is like the sun.

MY PEACE

Chapter Ten

Pax

I just lied to my wife.
　　I feel it in my gut.
　　All is not well. Not with me.
　　But I refuse to trouble Mila with it. I'm even more convinced of that now.
　　So I hold her hand, and stroke her hair, and ignore the pain in my leg, and I ignore the feeling of slipping down a hillside. I'm slipping, and I don't know how or why. I just know that I am.
　　I walk with her to our bedroom, and she stops to kiss Zuzu's forehead. Our daughter is sleeping peacefully, with her lamp on that makes stars dance on the ceiling. I turn it off.
　　"See? She's fine," I tell her. Mila smiles.
　　"She looks so much like Maddy."
　　I agree with that.
　　"I want this one to look like you," she adds. I shake my head.
　　"No way. Don't do that to the poor kid. It needs to look like you."
　　"You're beautiful and you know it," she argues. I tug her into the bedroom, and pull her shirt off.
　　"Let's get you into pajamas," I tell her. "Your favorite ones."

"Quit spoiling me. I'm fine."

I fold the blankets back, and she climbs in.

I get in beside her, pulling her close. Even after being at the hospital, she smells like sunshine.

"I don't know what I would do if something happened to you," I tell her honestly.

She looks up at me, her eyes wide and clear. "You don't have to worry about that. Not for a long, long time."

"I'm sorry I wasn't there when you called," I tell her. "It won't happen again."

"Babe, it's ok," she says and she closes her eyes, resting in my arms. "It's ok. Truly."

She's had a long day, and she sleeps soon.

But not me.

I lie awake, worrying about what could've happened. If she'd lost the baby, it would've crushed her.

My knee is throbbing, and I try to rub at it without disturbing Mila, but it isn't going to happen. The longer I lay in one spot, the more it seems to hurt. And when it hurts, it permeates every corner of my body. It doesn't stay in my leg.

I lie still for as long as I can take it, then I finally wiggle out of Mila's arms, and finagle my way to my feet. My knee threatens to give out again, but I steady myself, then limp down the hall to my study.

I stop only once, to poke my head inside Zu's bedroom. Her blond head rests peacefully on her pillow, her hand curled under her chin.

I continue on my way, and stop just inside the door, pouring myself a drink. I pour a second one, and take it with me across the room.

MY PEACE

Grimacing, I sit at my desk, and prop my leg up as best I can.

I let my head fall back, and I close my eyes, and Fuck, it hurts like a summabitch, as Gabe would say.

Mind over matter, I tell myself. *Mind over matter.*

But pain is a demanding mistress, and it refuses to be ignored.

"Again?" Natasha's voice fills the room, and I open my eyes.

She's concerned, in her robe again, and I nod.

"Yeah."

"You know, I was thinking. I have some muscle relaxers that my doctor gave me for my back. Do you want to try them? Maybe they could help."

She's hesitant, but she wants to help, and it's nice of her.

"Sure," I tell her. "I'll give anything a try at this point."

She smiles. "Ok. I'll be right back."

True to her word, she comes back within minutes, and hands me a bottle.

"Keep them all," she tells me. "I don't use them."

"Thank you." I gulp two down with whiskey. Natasha stares at me.

"I don't think you should take them with alcohol."

"I think I'll be fine. I weigh two-hundred pounds. These were prescribed for you, and you weigh... what... a hundred, soaking wet?"

"You flatter," she smiles.

I wasn't trying to.

"Should I make a doctor appointment for you tomorrow?" she asks. "I can be discreet, and Mrs. Tate won't know."

She almost sounds conspiratorial and I rush to set that straight.

"I don't like keeping things from Mila," I tell her. "I just don't want her to be worried. Especially after tonight."

"I understand completely," she answers. "I'll do my best to help you."

She glances down at my leg, and I realize that I'm in a t-shirt and boxer-briefs. It's almost indecent because you can see the bulge of my penis, but she doesn't seem to notice, thank God.

"Your knee is swollen," she points out. "I'll get you an icepack."

She's on her way out the door before I think to protest. When she comes back, she settles it on my leg, and damned, if it doesn't feel better.

"You should keep that iced," she advises. "The more it swells, the more it will hurt."

"That makes sense."

"You never said if you want me to make an appointment?"

I shake my head. "No. They're only going to tell me that I need surgery. There's nothing more they can do until then."

"So you're just going to grin and bear it?"

"Well, I doubt I'll be grinning, but yeah."

"Good night, Mr. Tate."

"Good night."

I sit with the night a while, staring out the windows. The grounds here are manicured and lush, and they are quiet

MY PEACE

now. I smile, thinking about how Zuzu and her future brothers and sisters will run and play in the gardens. They will have the childhood that I never had. Of that, I am sure.

I think about that for a minute, my childhood.

I spent it with my father, and I always thought he resented me, that he didn't like me.

But it turns out, that wasn't the case. He just really missed my mother.

And I miss her too. She died when I was young, but I haven't forgotten the way she smelled like honeysuckle, or the way she smiled at me like I was her whole world.

Mila is the kind of mother to Zuzu that my mother was to me. And I guess I just want her to have more chances to share that love. She's got so much of it to give. I'd give anything to keep her from harm.

I'd sacrifice anything.

I don't care if I fuck my leg up beyond all recognition and never walk again, Mila isn't going to lose this baby. Not if I can help it.

I realize that I might not be rational about all of this, but after the childhood I had, I must be given some slack. I'm not always rational.

I'm restless and even though the whiskey and muscle relaxers have taken the edge off, I still feel the pain. I rub at it, and climb to my feet, and limp out to the garage.

I scan the darkness, and in the last slot, my baby sits.

Danger, my '69 Charger.

I walk through the darkness and when I get to her, I pull her tarp off. She still gleams, midnight black, and I drop into her driver's seat. She's mint condition, and fuck, I love this car.

It brings back so many memories, of the life I had before, of meeting Mila, of times after that, when Mila and I would roar down the highway on hour-long drives. Her hand would be on my leg, and her hair would be blowing out the open window.

I smile at the memory.

I've been so blessed, so very fortunate.

I would've died years ago in this very car if it hadn't been for Mila.

She'd called the ambulance that saved my life.

I sprawl in the seat, and sit half in, and half out of the car. It smells like old leather in here, and it's so very familiar. As soon as my knee is healed, I'm going to drive this car.

Fuck being driven.

I listen to the radio for a bit, and then I'm startled by a voice.

"Mr. Tate?"

Jesus, is Natasha going to turn up everywhere I go?

"Hi, Natasha."

She bends down so she can see me.

"Are you ok?"

"Yes. I was... reminiscing."

"Maybe you should go to bed," she suggests. "You're going to be so tired tomorrow."

I stare at her. "Did you boss my grandfather around, too?"

She's sheepish now. "I took care of your grandfather, yes. He liked it that way."

The way she says that strikes me oddly. "You didn't... I mean, you and he weren't..."

MY PEACE

She visibly shrinks back. "Oh, my lord. No. I viewed him like a father. That's all. I wanted to take care of him because he worked so hard and rarely took care of himself."

"Calm down," I tell her, and I can't help but smile. The whiskey and muscle relaxers have made me zen. More so than I've been in awhile. "I didn't mean any offense."

She stiffens her shoulders. "Being with Mr. Alexander wouldn't be an insult," she tells me. "It would be an honor."

"He was fifty years older than you," I point out.

She shrugs.

"Mr. Tate, you're changing the subject. I really think you should rest."

"And I really think you shouldn't worry about it," I tell her. "I'm fine."

"You have a full schedule tomorrow."

"And how would you know about that?"

"Sasha sends me your schedule every evening for the following day. It's how your grandfather did it."

"Huh. So if I forget something, I can ask you?"

"Exactly."

"That will come in handy," I admit. "What do I have tomorrow?"

"You have a meeting with Peter at eight a.m."

I picture Peter's stern face and pinched nose.

"Fuck."

"So, bed then?" she asks brightly, holding out her hand to help me up. I growl at her, but she's right. I sigh.

"Yeah."

She hefts me out of the car, and I even lean on her a little as we climb the handful of stairs leading out of the garage. My leg feels heavy and awkward, and I almost use her as a crutch. Something about her feels familiar, and it makes me comfortable. I can't put my finger on it.

We're just coming through the doorway when Mila bumps into us.

She's wearing a robe, her hair is disheveled, and she's horrified.

And that's when I realize how this must look.

MY PEACE

Chapter Eleven

Mila

I stare aghast at my husband, who is walking arm in arm with our new house-keeper out of a darkened garage. She's wearing a robe, and he's wearing a t-shirt and underwear.

"This isn't what it looks like," Pax says quickly, and my heart… it thumps so loudly in my chest that I think he can probably hear it.

"No?" I ask, and my lips seem to be frozen.

"No," Natasha stammers. "I just knew Mr. Tate was up, and so I went to check on him, and…"

"You went to check on him in the garage?" I ask, and I know I sound cold, but the girl is still holding onto my husband's arm. She sees my gaze and releases him.

"Yes, m'am," she acknowledges. "In the garage."

"I was sitting in Danger," Pax tells me, and I think he actually looks pale. "I was listening to the radio. I couldn't sleep. I didn't want to wake you. And why are you out of bed?"

"Because you were gone," I tell him evenly. "And you didn't come back. I waited for an hour, and then decided to come looking for you."

"God, I'm sorry, babe," he tells me and he touches my arm. I back away.

"Pax, why were you and Natasha holding onto each other, if it's not what it looks like?"

He takes a breath, and when he does, when he exhales, I smell it.

Whiskey.

"Were you out there drinking?" I ask him, astounded. Because what the hell?

"No," he rushes to tell me. "I had a drink in my office, hoping to settle down, but I wasn't drinking out in the garage. I just... I missed my car so I went to sit in her."

"With Natasha," I say slowly.

"No. Natasha came to check on me. I wasn't *with* Natasha."

I'm still and I don't know what to think and I'm not supposed to be walking around.

"I'm going back to bed," I tell him. Natasha looks helpless and Pax is flustered. He trails next to me, and that's when I realize that he's limping again.

"Your knee is still bothering you," I point out, turning to him.

"Just a little," he answers. "Don't worry about it, babe. Let's go back to bed. You have to rest."

I turn, and wordlessly walk the rest of the way and I notice that I have to slow down for Pax to keep up.

"You need to go back to the doctor," I tell him.

He shakes his head. "It's not necessary right now, Red. Trust me."

I climb back into the cool sheets and Pax lies down beside me.

"You swear to God nothing was going on with Natasha?"

I hate the suspicious tone in my voice. He's never given me a reason to doubt him. Not ever. But I think any

MY PEACE

wife would question her husband coming out of a darkened garage with another woman in the middle of the night.

"I swear to God," he says firmly. "Lord. Why would I want anyone else when I have you?"

"Well, I am pretty perfect," I quip, relaxing. "I guess you'd be crazy."

"I might be crazy," he tells me. "But I'm not stupid. You're the best thing that's ever happened to me, and I'm not losing you. Not ever."

"So you weren't doing anything with Natasha?" I can't help myself.

"God, no." He's firm and immediate.

"Ok."

I curl onto my side, and close my eyes. But I open them a minute later.

"Pax?"

"Yeah, babe?"

"Please don't sit in a dark car with her again."

"Promise."

I grip his arm in my hands, and his muscle bulges beneath my fingertips.

"You're mine."

"I'm yours," he agrees. "There is no question about that."

"Good."

***

When I wake, Pax is gone. I must've been sleeping so hard that he didn't want to wake me. It feels odd though, to start my day without kissing my husband.

When I go into the bathroom though, there's a note taped to my mirror.

Babe, I love you. ONLY YOU. See you soon!

I can't help but smile at that, and warmth floods my belly.

It's weird how night-time makes a person think different thoughts than they would in the light of day. Pax would never betray me. Not ever. I know that.

Grimacing, I head back to bed.

I don't want to, but I know that I can't get up for a week.

Zuzu runs in to cuddle as soon as she's asleep and shortly after, Chelcie arrives.

"Pax called me," she says brightly, and she opens the drapes. "I'll be here every day this week to look after Zu."

"Thank you," I tell her gratefully. "I'll only be down for a week."

"And I'm also supposed to make sure you stay down," she tells me ruefully. "Sorry."

I roll my eyes. "That's ok. I'd expect nothing less out of Pax. I'm surprised he hasn't stationed National Guard soldiers at my door."

"Don't give him ideas," she cautions. "I'm going to take Zu to the zoo today, if that's ok with you. There's a new otter exhibit. I think she'll love it."

My heart twinges because I'd love to take her to that, but I can't be selfish. I don't want her sitting at home worrying about her mama.

"That's fine," I tell her. Zuzu is excited, and kisses me goodbye, and when they leave, my room is so quiet.

I'm so bored.

MY PEACE

I text Maddy and Pax. I pick up a book. I scan through channels.

I wasn't made to lie still.

It's an hour or so before Natasha knocks softly, then pokes her head in.

"M'am?"

Even though I know Pax wasn't doing anything with her, something about her grates at me.

"Yes?"

"I came to see what you want for breakfast."

She is subdued.

"Scrambled eggs and fruit would be lovely," I answer. I force myself to be friendly. She hasn't done anything to me. My instincts are clouded by my pregnant hormones.

"Coming right up," she says, and she smiles. "Can I get anything for you?"

"Yes, actually. If you could get my hairbrush from the bathroom, I'd really appreciate it."

"Of course." She scampers in to get it, and I try to pretend to myself that I didn't send her in there to see Pax's note which is still taped on the mirror. It takes her a couple of minutes, and I'm sure she's reading it.

I don't know what's come over me, but I'm satisfied by that. I've never been jealous before.

When she re-emerges with my hairbrush, she is nonplussed, and on her way out the door, I call after her.

"Could you grab a sketch pad on your way back? I'm dying of boredom."

"Of course," she nods, and she's gone.

Her perfume lingers though, and it's sweet, floral. I try to put my finger on what it is. Jasmine? No.

Rose? No.

It's not until he comes back with my breakfast that I decide.

It's honeysuckle.

MY PEACE

Chapter Twelve

Pax

Work is uneventful, even the dreaded meeting with Peter first thing in the morning.

By afternoon, I'm tired again. The lack of sleep thing is taking its toll.

At three o'clock, Sasha buzzes me.

"Mr. Tate, you have a phone call."

"From?"

She hesitates. "From the Marion Correctional Facility."

My heart thuds dully in my chest, because Leroy Ellison is there.

The son-of-a bitch who killed my mother.

"Put him through," I tell her, and my voice is like wood, and what the hell is that fucker calling me?

"Hello?"

An elderly man is in my ear, and I haven't heard this voice in a long, long time.

"What do you want?"

There's a laugh now, and it sounds wet, like he needs to cough.

"Well, now, son. Is that any way to greet your long lost Uncle Leroy?"

"Shut the fuck up," I tell him. "Why are you calling me?"

"Do you still have your X, kid? His voice is so craggy and I look at the base of my thumb, where it meets my hand. A jagged scar in the shape on an X is there, carved by Leroy's knife so long ago, right after he killed my mother.

X marks the spot.

"I can still find you, you know," he adds.

I wait.

"You know you're the one who bumped the trigger. I shouldn't be here. It should be you."

"You son of a bitch," I spit. "I was a kid, and you were forcing yourself on my mother. I was trying to save her."

"Regardless," he continues, as they he doesn't have a care in the world. "I shouldn't be here. Think on that."

He hangs up, and I'm stunned.

What the hell was that all about?

I'm in shock as I sit in my rich leather chair and stare out the wall of windows to my left. Below me, Hartford bustles around on it's busy streets and I suddenly feel all alone.

My mother's killer called me at work. So he somehow knows that I'm working here, and probably knows my grandfather is dead.

Of course, he could've gotten that from the newspapers.

He must not have much to do in prison.

I'm suddenly burning with rage that he would dare to contact me. What gives him the right to even fucking speak to me?

I pick up the phone to call Mila, because that's what I would normally do. We share everything.

MY PEACE

Only… today… Mila is at home in bed with our unborn child, trying to ensure that it lives.

She's got more to worry about than an old dumbass who is sitting in prison trying to get a rise out of me. I put my phone back down.

I'll tell her about it later. Next week, when she's up and around again.

With a sigh, I try to call my father instead, but he's in a meeting.

Fuck, the adult world sucks sometimes.

I focus on work documents, scanning contracts, rubbing my knee.

And then, right before I decide to close-up shop to go home, Sasha comes in with the mail.

"It's late today," she tells me, as she puts the pre-opened stack in my inbox. She opens them, scans them, and flags them for me, categorized by color. Yellow means it can wait, Green means it needs a signature, and Red means it's very important, and those are on top.

I only have one red flag today.

Sitting back in my chair, I grab it.

It's a letter.

My eyes are glued to it as I read it from start to end, the scrawling handwriting clearly masculine.

Pax,

I hope this letter finds you well.

I think you'll be interested in what I have to say, it you give me a few minutes to say it.

Would you like to know what your mother said to me about you before she died?

I'm the only one who knows, and I can tell you.

The price is small.

Best regards,

Leroy H. Ellison

My breath hitches in my throat and I read it again, then again.

The envelope is clipped to the letter by a paper clip, and it is stamped INMATE CORRESPONDENCE.

Son of a bitch.

I don't know what to do. All I know is what I want to do, and that is drive to the Marion prison and punch this fucking guy's throat in.

What. The. Fuck.

I can't even think clearly.

I stalk out of the office, knowing that Sasha will call for the car. I'm right. Roger is waiting at front doors to usher me into the back.

"Home, sir?" he asks as he climbs in the driver's seat.

"No. Drive around for a while, please. I need to clear my thoughts."

"You got it."

The limo noses out of the lot into the street, and I stare absently out the window, at the traffic, at the trees, at the people walking on the sidewalk.

I should put Leroy Ellison out of my head.

There's nothing he can offer me that makes speaking with him worth it.

Except... what had my mother said?

It doesn't matter. She's gone now, and probably anything he says would be a lie. I can't trust him. I know that. As I think, I rub at the scar on my hand, the scar he gave me, back when I was a little boy and couldn't fight back.

I'd watched him sexually violate my mother when I was shoved into the closet, and then... well, she'd died.

I don't know what, if anything, she said in between. I was in the closet, hiding like the scared little boy I was.

What had she said?

Damn it. I'm pissed because this is exactly how he wants me to feel, and I don't want to play into his hands.

I'm not going to play into his hands.

I'm not.

Fuck him.

Nothing my mother said will change the fact that she's gone.

I pull out the bottle of muscle relaxers that Natasha gave me and toss a couple into my mouth. Then, I wait. The pain dulls, relaxation comes. They must be pretty strong, because it happens quickly and brings with it a rush of dizziness.

"We can go home now."

Roger turns toward home, and the drive goes quickly, because he's taking me to my wife.

I climb out, and I'm through the door, and I'm down the hall, ignoring the pain of walking, ignoring the bullshit from Leroy, and I'm walking through the bedroom doors, and Mila is smiling at me.

She's in the bed where she's supposed to be, and her face lights up when I enter the room.

"Babe," she exclaims. "I missed you."

My heart floods with warmth, and everything melts away when I see her. She's everything. She's all I need.

I sit next to her, gathering her into my arms.

"You feel skinnier," I fret. "Are you eating?"

"Yes," she nods. "A lot."

"Are you resting?"

"Yes. You've got Natasha, Chelcie *and* Maddy checking on me. I couldn't go anywhere if I tried."

I pull her to me, inhaling her skin, my lips pressed to her neck. Lavender, vanilla, and everything good. That's what she smells like. Sunshine and rain, earth and the sun. I hold her close, gripping her tight. She threads her fingers through my hair, and then she pulls back a little.

"Are you ok?" she asks gently. "What's wrong, babe?"

"Nothing," I lie. "Nothing at all. Everything is ok."

It does seem to be, when I am with her. It's corny as hell, but true.

"Zuzu and I were just getting ready to have a picnic in here," Mila tells me. "For dinner. It seemed like you might be late, so I wanted to feed her."

"I brought plenty," Natasha says as she comes in the door with a giant basket and my daughter. Zu bounds into my arms, bouncing on the bed.

"Calm down, sweet," I tell her. "You can't jostle mommy around right now."

"Because of the baby in her tummy?"

My gaze flies to Mila and she shrugs. "Natasha didn't realize that Zu didn't know. The cat is out of the bag."

"I'm so sorry," Natasha tells me. "I can't believe I was so dumb."

"It's ok," Mila tells her, and I can tell it's not the first time Natasha has apologized. "She had to know eventually."

"I'm going to have a sister," Zu tells me seriously.

"Or a brother," I answer. "One or the other."

MY PEACE

"It's a sister," she says confidently. "I know it."

Mila and I laugh, and our entire family is on this bed. Natasha pauses at the foot.

"Hop down, sweetheart," she tells Zuzu. "I'm going to set up dinner."

And she does. She spreads a picnic tablecloth and lays out a picnic spread befitting of a royal family.

"This is lovely," Mila tells her, reaching for a piece of cheese. "Thank you."

"It's my pleasure."

Natasha breezes past me and out the door, and I once again feel like I know her, but I don't know from where.

It doesn't matter.

I'm with Mila and Zuzu now. That's what matters.

We eat, the cold fried chicken and the biscuits and the cheese. I feed Zuzu pieces of grapes and Mila licks her fingers.

"This is perfect," she says happily.

"Are you doing ok? No pain?" I ask her. She shakes her head.

"No pain, no blood. Stop worrying."

"As if."

She shakes her head, and I look at our daughter, who is already yawning.

"Chelsea took her to the zoo," Mila explains. "She's worn out."

"I'll get her ready for bed," I tell her. "Seven o'clock isn't too early, is it?"

"Not for such a long day," she answers. "Thank you."

I read Zuzu her favorite book twice, then turn on her lamp. I tuck her favorite stuffed tiger in next to her and kiss her forehead.

Then I head back to Mila.

"I'm going to take a shower, then join you," I tell her.

"I'm looking forward to it."

I let the hot water pour down on me, and put most of the weight on my good leg. The steam builds up and drains most of my tension, and by the time I towel off, I feel much better.

To be on the safe side, I pop a couple more muscle relaxers before I join my wife in bed.

She welcomes me with open arms, and I mold my body to hers, because this is where I belong.

Chapter Thirteen

My father flies into town two days later and meets me after work at the Pub.

"What exactly did he say?" he asks me seriously. His hands twist together, because if anyone hates Leroy Ellison more than I do, it's my father.

"He said it should be me in prison, and that he wanted to tell me something mom said."

"He doesn't know shit," my father swears, and picks up his whiskey glass. "Don't pay him any mind."

"I know," I tell him, and I gulp my drink too. "I just wonder… I mean, *did* she say anything?"

"If she did, it wasn't anything we didn't already know. Your mother always communicated her feelings. She even left those letters for you in case anything ever happened to her. She was always prepared, always spoke her mind. Trust me."

"Yeah, I guess you're right," I admit, and I drain my glass. My father narrows his eyes.

"I haven't seen you drink like this in a long time. You ok?"

I signal the bartender for another. "Just a lot of stress right now. I'm fine. No reason to worry."

"Ok," he says hesitantly, and for a minute, I see the old concern in his eyes, the concern he used to have back when I was using drugs and disappearing into a bottle of Jack.

"I'm fine," I reassure him. "I've got a handle on things. There's just a lot right now."

"I know," he sympathizes. "I know. If you need me again, I'm just a phone call away."

"That and a thousand miles."

"More like eight hundred. No distance is too great though, son."

My father has truly embraced showing his feelings nowadays. Sometimes, I like it. Sometimes, it makes me uncomfortable.

"Do you have time to come over to the house?"

He shakes his head. "Unfortunately, I don't tonight. I'll come back next week or so."

"Ok."

We finish our drinks, and he shakes my hand, then hugs me. He leaves, and I head to the restroom. While I'm standing at the urinal, I'm hit with an overwhelming desire to use.

It comes from nowhere, like a great black wave, and I can taste heroin in my mouth, I can feel it pulsing in my blood. I can feel the sting of the needle, and I can smell the it in my nostrils. It's sharp, it's overwhelming.

I fight to breathe around the feeling, but the breath doesn't want to come.

"Dude, you alright?" the guy next to me asks, his dick in his hand. He's breaking bro-code to ask.

"Yeah."

I put one hand on the wall, finish my piss, and finally manage to breathe.

What the actual fuck?

The craving doesn't go away, and it is still there on the ride home.

MY PEACE

I open the muscle relaxers and swallow four of them, lying my head back against the seat, gritting my teeth.

This can't be happening.

I won't use.

This isn't a part of my life anymore.

But holy shit. The need... for heroin, for cocaine... it's overtaking me right now. It's coursing through me, tangible and real. I almost feel shaky with it.

And I don't know why.

Son of a bitch.

My skin is clammy and cold, and when we pull up to the front doors of my home, and Roger opens my door, I'm not ready to get out.

I'm still too shaky.

But I put on a brave front, and step into my home, because I'm not a god-damned pussy and I am stronger than this.

Whatever *this* is.

I'm surprised to see Mila up and about, with a cup of hot cocoa in her hand. I stand still, prepared to lecture, and she grins.

"My doctor said I could get up. He gave me the all clear!"

She's radiant, absolutely glowing.

"You're sure?" I ask. "It's not dangerous?"

"No," she says firmly. "He says I'm fine. The baby is fine. I can resume life as normal. If any other bleeding happens, I'm supposed to let him know, of course, but I'm fine, babe. Please stop worrying now."

We've only got a couple of weeks until she passes the first trimester mark.

My knee throbs as a reminder.

I'll take care of it as soon as possible. In a couple of weeks.

"This calls for a celebration," I tell her. "Let's go out to eat."

"Natasha is already making us a fancy dinner," she tells me. "And Zu is spending the night with Maddy. She was watching her while I was at the doctor's, and she asked if she could keep her."

"Why didn't you tell me you had an appointment?" I ask.

"Because I didn't want you to worry."

Her answer is simple, and she is so like me in that way. She'd rather bear bad news alone, and shield me from it the best she can.

It's the same thing I'm doing for her.

"Tell Natasha to serve it in the living room," I tell her. "And you'll be eating in my lap."

I scoop her up and she giggles the entire way to the living room. When we get there, I've changed my mind.

"Fuck it," I mutter. "Tell her to keep it warm."

Mila giggles the message into her cellphone, and I deposit her in the middle of the bed. I strip off my shirt and pants, and then kneel over her, peeling off her clothing items one by one. I pull her panties off with my teeth.

Her smell, musky and fresh, floods my nose and I'm instantly hard.

Her hands are everywhere on my skin, pulling me to her, and her heat… Jesus, her heat engulfs me, and I cover her with my body.

My lips blaze a trail from her belly to her mouth, and mouth is needy.

"I want you," she tells me urgently. "Please, Pax."

MY PEACE

Her legs are looped around my hips already and I have to mentally slow down. I want it to last. I don't want to hurt her.

I feel her, every inch of her, palming her in my hands and playing her like an instrument. She arches and whimpers, and I smile, her lips against my teeth.

"Tell me what you want, Red," I urge her.

"You," she whispers daintily. "You."

"What part of me?" I ask, knowing damned well what she wants. "Tell me, Red. Say it."

"I want your hard cock," her sweet mouth says, and the dirty words sound so good coming from her delicate lips.

I give it to her. I slide into her, from tip to base, and I shudder with the ecstasy of it. She whimpers and clutches at my back, and I slow myself down again.

Dead puppies, nuns, cold fish. I calm myself, and rhythmically, gently, I fuck my wife.

She grasps the sheets, she clutches at my hips, her legs are tight, her pussy is tighter.

"Dear Lord," she says into my chest.

"Don't bring him into this," I tell her, and I groan as I thrust deeper. I pull myself back. I can't hurt her. I can't.

"I'm not made of glass," she tells me weakly, and she pulls me further into her, and it's my undoing.

I shudder, and convulse, and my hot fluid fills her up.

I hold myself above her, making sure I don't crush her. Her face is buried in my shoulder, and I think she's crying.

I look at her quickly, and she is, but she's shaking her head not to worry.

"It's my hormones," she finally says. "I'm happy, babe."

Relieved, I roll off and hold her, and she sniffles. "I never thought I'd be so happy," says.

"Me, too," I agree. "Never."

But even still, as we bask in the afterglow of making love, the rumblings of my cravings come back. They wind their way out of my gut, out of the blackness and the void, and into my thoughts, my chest.

I suck in air because it hits me so hard yet again, out of the blue.

It's like wind taking the sails of a ship. It grabs hold and flies.

I take a deep breath, and will the awfulness away, and how can I even be feeling like this with my wife in my arms? I've not needed to use even once since I've been with her. She's been everything I needed.

Why is this rearing its head now?

I ponder what to do while we make our way to the dining room to eat, and we sit side by side. Mila grips my thigh between bites, and her hand is warm and mine.

But she can't make the craving go away.

It's planted in my head, and it won't leave me alone.

I feed my wife dessert while hiding my struggle. I laugh at her jokes, but I don't feel the amusement. I'm empty inside for this moment, because all I can do is crave.

It's eating at me.

Overwhelming me.

It makes no sense.

It makes no sense.

Long after Mila is sleeping, tucked safely into our bed, I find my way to my study.

It's the middle of the night, and I can't think around my need to use.

MY PEACE

It comes in waves, big waves.

I dump the rest of the pill bottle into my hand, and chew them up, swallowing the bitterness without flinching.

I feel instant relief, as the ground up powder enters my bloodstream through my stomach, and I close my eyes, letting it dull the need.

The need is a monster, and I just made a blood offering.

It will be quiet now, for a little while.

I fall asleep on the sofa in my study.

Chapter Fourteen

Mila

I wake with a stretch, the sun on my face, and Pax is gone.

I know this because my fingers brush against cool sheets, instead of his warm body.

I glance at the clock. Eight o'clock. He's at work. He didn't wake me, that rascal.

I leisurely shower and blow-dry my hair, and then text Maddy.

What time should I come get Zu?

She answers immediately. *Can I bring her home after lunch?*

Ok, I answer.

She's probably taking her shoe shopping again.

My stomach growls and I decide the baby needs to eat. I make my way down the hall to the kitchen, but on my way, I pass Pax's study, and there is movement inside.

Pausing in the doorway, I see Natasha hovering above Pax, giving him a glass of water and pills.

"What the hell?"

I didn't mean to sound so sharp, but seriously.

They both look up at me and Pax's eyes are bloodshot.

"I'm sorry, babe. I couldn't sleep last night and I fell asleep in here. Natasha just brought me some aspirin."

MY PEACE

"Why couldn't you sleep?" I ask curiously, practically nudging past Natasha to examine him. I put my hand on his forehead. "You don't have a fever, but you look rough."

"I don't know,' he tells me, but he's troubled. I can see it in his hazel eyes and they are so green right now. That's what happens when he's troubled. They're green as moss, like a murky pond, hiding things in their depths.

"Natasha, can you excuse us for a minute? I ask.

"Of course," she exits immediately.

"What's happening?" I ask my husband, sitting next to him. "You're sleeping in your study, you're late for work." I glance at the bar, and there is a scotch bottle out, and a used tumbler. "And you seem to be drinking a lot."

"I'm just stressed, babe," he tells me and he is so earnest, so genuine, but even still... there's something. I feel it.

"No lies," I tell him. "You promised me that once. You promised never to lie to me again. Remember?"

"Of course," he answers sharply. "Of course I do."

"Then why are you lying?" I ask simply.

His face contorts and his hand clenches in his lap. A vein pulses in his temple, the one that pops out when he's furious.

"I'm not lying," he snaps, and he's suddenly so angry. "Why would you accuse me of something like that?"

His sudden anger seems out of proportion for the current situation. I stare at him, hesitant. I don't know what to say.

"You feel different," I say finally. "I don't know how to explain it. You're edgy right now. Like a caged lion."

I wait, and he sighs.

"My knee hurts," he tells me finally. Reluctantly. "It needs surgery."

I gasp, and stare at him, and he nods.

"It's ok. I just didn't want to worry you until you were out of the woods with the baby. I don't want you to worry. It'll just be quick surgery and they'll fix me up."

"And in the meantime, you're in excruciating pain?" I guess. He looks away.

"A bit."

"Pax! Oh my God. This was so unnecessary. You didn't have to keep this from me. I swear to God, sometimes you're protective to a fault. You need to make an appointment today for surgery. No more delays. I'm fine. Do it."

He stares at me, searching my face, and then he finally nods.

"If you're sure."

"Oh my God," I swear. "Do it."

"Ok." He's sheepish now, and I'm glad.

"Seriously. I can't believe you did this."

"Calm down," he tells me, standing. He's wobbly, and his knee gives out. He tries again, this time successful.

"Are you even supposed to be walking on it?" I eye it doubtfully.

He doesn't answer, which is answer enough.

"Call today," I tell him firmly.

"I will."

He dresses and heads to work, and I have breakfast.

When Natasha comes to clear my dishes, she pauses.

"I'm so sorry I didn't tell you about his knee," she apologizes. "But he didn't want you to know."

My head snaps up at this.

MY PEACE

"You knew?"

She nods. "Yeah. He's been having trouble sleeping, and I've caught him up and around the house at night. He's been in a lot of pain. But he didn't want to worry you."

Natasha knew.

For some reason, this bothers me. He told Natasha, our housekeeper, but not me? That seems very, very wrong. Very, very unlike him.

"Well, thank you for taking care of him," I finally say limply. She nods again, pleased with herself.

"Of course. I took care of his grandfather, and I'm happy to take care of Mr. Tate, as well."

Except taking care of Mr. Tate is *my* job. But I don't point that out.

Instead, I fiddle around the house, messing around in my new studio, trying to arrange my supplies, but my agitation over the situation blocks my creativity. I can't seem to focus on drawing or painting.

When Maddy comes in, she brings the mail, and hands it to Natasha, who whisks it away for sorting. There is a small box addressed to Pax on top, but it's gone before I see what it is.

My daughter distracts me anyway.

"Mama!" she shrieks, throwing herself into my arms and holding out her foot. "Look at my new boots!"

"I knew it," I roll my eyes at my sister. "Mad, I seriously am running out of room to put her shoes."

"In this house?" she's doubtful. "You should make her a walk-in closet out of a room you don't use. That's every girl's dream."

I chuckle. "Maybe it's *your* dream."

"It's every girl's dream," she assures me. "You should do it. You'd be a super-hero to her."

"I'm a super-hero to her already," I tell her. "Until she turns thirteen or so."

We visit for a while, and Maddy finally stares at me. "What's wrong with you? You should be on Cloud Nine since you can get up and around now."

I pause, and consider, and finally tell her my concerns about Natasha.

"I don't have any grounds for it," I finish up finally. "I just feel uncomfortable with her around my husband. I feel like... I don't know."

Maddy nods seriously. "I've honestly had a bad feeling about her all along," she says and thank God for sisters who always understand. "I really have. There's something... I can't put my finger on it. But what woman her age wants to be the housekeeper to an old man like Pax's grandfather? I mean, she doted on him. I wonder if there was something there?"

I shudder at that. "Surely not." But then I think on it. "Maybe she wanted his money?"

Maddy nods. "Maybe. And who has his money now?"

I'm silent. Pax does. We do.

"Son of a bitch," I finally mutter. Maddy nods again.

"Money brings problems with it," she says, and I have to agree.

"But we could be wrong about her," I muse aloud.

"We could be," my sister agrees. "But I don't think so. We have instincts for a reason. To use them."

"We can't fire her," I tell her. "We have to keep her on staff for five years."

MY PEACE

"But you could move her away from you," Maddy suggests. "Just think about it."

"I will."

And I will. I hate to be unfair, and I hope I'm not being unfair right now. But my life is my life, and no one will protect it but me.

At this moment, a text comes in from Pax.

I love you.

I smile and text him back. *I love you, too.*

Chapter Fifteen
Pax

I sit at my desk, and finally, I look up my doctor's number.

I speak with the nurse.

"I'd like to schedule the surgery for my knee please."

"When looks good for you, Mr. Tate?"

"The earlier, the better. It's causing a bit of pain."

As in, excruciating, debilitating pain.

She's silent as she looks through the schedule.

"Well, Dr. Talbot is on vacation for the next two weeks, but Dr. Otham could do the surgery if you'd like?"

"Uh. I don't know Dr. Otham," I tell her.

"I assure you, he's quite good. He could fit you in next week."

"But if I wait one more week after that, I can have my regular doctor?"

She checks.

"Yes. Dr. Talbot can do it the week he returns."

"Let's do that."

"Ok." She puts me on the calendar, and I put it on mine. When I hang on, I count the days.

Eighteen days.

I call her back.

"Can I have some muscle relaxers to help with the pain in the meantime?"

She pauses. "Muscle relaxers won't help with this, Mr. Tate." The hell they won't. I want to tell her I've been taking them, but don't. "And I'm not sure, given your history, that Dr. Talbot will want to prescribe you anything stronger. I'll check with him and get back to you."

"Don't bother."

I hang up on her. *My history?* Why the fuck had I been so honest in filling out my medical history when I became a patient? They're just using my honesty against me, and now I'm stuck with pain.

The pain swells as the minutes pass, and eventually, it's all I can think about. Rubbing it doesn't help. I'm drowning in an ocean of misery. The hair at the back of my neck is damp with trying to control it. It's not working.

Finally, with shaking hands, I pull out the empty pill bottle from where I'd stuck it in my desk. Why I hadn't thrown it away, I don't know.

I examine the label.

Two refills remaining.

I wonder if Natasha would mind?

I text her.

She answers immediately. *Of course not! Go right ahead. I can pick them up, if you want.*

That would be great, I tell her. *Can you drop them off with Sasha?*

Because I need them now.

Fuck their "with your history" bullshit. It's been five years since I've used anything at all. They don't know shit about me.

I can't focus well on work, but I try.

A couple hours later, Sasha comes in with the pills, and she brings me a giant gel ice-pack, too.

"Natasha suggested it," she tells me when I look at it strangely. "I have another one in the freezer when this one gets warm. Just yell at me."

"Thanks," I tell her, my fingers wrapping around the new pill bottle. They are more precious than gold to me right now.

I am antsy for her to leave, and when she does, I swallow four pills, after chewing them. It makes them hit my bloodstream faster, and God, when they do... sweet relief.

It doesn't take the pain away completely, but it takes the edge off and makes it bearable.

An hour later, Mila texts.

Did you call the doctor?

Yes, babe. Surgery in a couple of weeks.

Thank God! She answers. *I love you.*

It's only been an hour, but I take another pill.

I've got to pace myself, I know, but they help. They really do. They seem to make my mind fuzzy, too, and for some reason, right now, I like that. It also distracts me from the pain.

I put the bottle away, and don't even look at it again until I leave for the day.

I take another pill in the car.

That leave twenty-four in the bottle. And then one more refill of thirty pills.

I make a mental note.

This blown-out knee business is no-joke.

I notice that Roger isn't taking me toward home, and I ask him about it.

"Oh, sorry sir. Your wife instructed me to take you to her instead."

MY PEACE

"And where is she?" I feel stupid having to ask.

"She's waiting for you for dinner."

"So, it's a surprise, then?" I'm wry now. My wife loves random surprises.

"Yes, sir."

I sit back and wait, and it's not too terribly long before we're pulling through the gates of a park on the outside of town. The car glides silently along the quiet street until we stop in front of a glistening lake.

There are Japanese lanterns hung from here to the water, where a fancy tent is set up, and my wife waits by the doors. I know she did all of this herself. It's not like her to ask the staff. So she and Maddy must've worked all afternoon.

Not only that, but she looks stunning in a black cocktail dress, simple and snug. It fits her perfectly. Her hair cascades down her back, and I can see her smile from here.

I'm already grinning as I walk down the softly lit path, and when I reach my wife, I kiss her hard.

"Welcome to dinner," she tells me softly, and my hands glide up under her dress to her perfect ass.

"Ah-ah-ah. Not yet. First, I feed you."

She pulls away, and I examine the tent. Silk drapes everything, and cushions cover the floor. It looks like something out of a middle-eastern harem, fancy and expensive. It's inviting, and all I really want to do is lay my wife down on the silk and fuck her.

But.

I don't.

Instead, I sit on the cushions and eat with her.

A magnificent picnic is laid in front of us, and I try not to show the pain I'm feeling from getting down on the ground. I don't want her to know the extent of it.

Hanging lanterns with candles in them surround us, and the whole thing is something out of a movie.

"Where did you get this idea?" I ask her as I bite into a hot buttered roll.

"A book I'm reading," she answers. "Do you like it?"

"Yes." I glance over her shoulder and there is a bed-shaped area behind her. "I can't help but notice there is a bed here."

"Um-hmm," she nods. "We have to have dessert, don't we?"

My heart swells three sizes. "You know me well."

"I know that while you tolerate chocolate cake, you'd much rather lick me for dessert," she agrees. "I do know you."

I can't eat my dinner fast enough knowing what awaits me. I'm not even worried that a passerby will hear the noise coming from the tent. To be fair, I've never worried much about what others might think.

I stand up carefully while Mila is still eating. I want her attention to be focused elsewhere, rather than on my troubles. I manage, and while I'm at it, I untie the silk cord holding open the door. It closes, and we have instant privacy.

Stepping carefully, I head to the bed area.

Mila follows, and when I'm on my back, she smiles, stripping her dress off.

She's not wearing a bra or underwear.

I suck in my breath and stare at her and she is so beautiful that my gut hurts with it.

MY PEACE

"I'm going to blindfold you now," she says sweetly, pulling a black satin scarf out of a cushion.

I raise an eyebrow. "So I can't see you? *Dislike.*"

She smiles. "Oh, you'll *like.* Trust me."

"I have no doubt."

Obediently, I tie the scarf around my eyes.

"Can you see?" Mila's voice is low, next to my ear, and I can feel her nipples grazing my arm. I reach out to the cup them, and she pulls away.

"You didn't think it would be that easy, did you? Lie still, babe."

She ties my feet—each foot to something. And then my hands—above my head.

"Hmm. What do you have planned for me?" I ask. "Will I be gagged next?

She chuckles. "No. I need your mouth free and clear."

She straddles my hips, and the moistness between her legs is next to my skin. It's enough to spring my dick to life, and it pushes against her, hot and hard.

"Awww, you like me," she points out with a laugh.

"Let me show you how much," I suggest. She laughs again.

"In good time. For now, I have something for you to suck."

She presses her full breasts against my mouth, and eagerly, I pull her nipples in, sucking at the pinkness, licking, lapping, then sucking again. It's just how she likes it, and even though I'm the one who is bound, she's the one who is moaning.

"You like?" I ask against her lips, and my voice is husky. I want her already. My wife knows just what to do to make me crazy.

"Oh, I do," she assures me. "But you're not finished yet. You have to work for your dinner."

She straddles my face, and her muskiness is all around me, and I breathe it in. She's wet and warm and God, she's delicious. I lick at her, making circles with my tongue before I plunge it back inside of her. I fuck her with it, over and over, licking, sucking, fucking. Even though I can't see, I know she's limp. I can feel it.

I want to cup her ass with my hands, but I'm restrained. I chafe at my ties, but they won't budge. Mila laughs.

"Nope."

She un-straddles me, and then she's gone... but she's back soon enough. Her mouth is running up and down the length of my hard shaft, and I suck in a deep breath.

"Jesus."

She breathes onto me, hot and moist, and my dick throbs hard inside her mouth. She glides along the shaft, then slips the head into her mouth, sucking sucking sucking, and then she's out again... and licking at my balls. She sucks them lightly, just how I like it, and good lord, I don't think I've ever wanted to be inside her more than I do at this moment.

"Please, babe," I tell her. "Please let me be inside of you."

And just like that, she carefully straddles me again, careful not to jar my knee, and I'm plunging deep inside of her. She takes all of me on the first plunge, and I groan with the pure ecstasy of it. There's nothing like that first plunge, hot and wet and tight.

I swallow hard, and she rocks gently, then more and more forcefully… quicker and quicker, and then she gives me sweet release.

I groan as I spurt inside of her, and her muscles clench, as though she's trying to suck it all up, trying to take it all and keep it.

"God," I finally say. "You're so fucking hot, babe."

"I'm glad you think so," she says in satisfaction and she unties my blindfold.

"Are you ok?" I ask her quickly. "No blood?"

She nods. "I'm fine. No blood."

Relief rushes through me, and I notice that my knee is throbbing again. I'd strained against it more than I'd thought because I was distracted by the ecstasy of sex. Now that it's finished, the pain is emerging, worse than ever.

Son of a bitch.

"Let's get you home," she tells me as she unties my hands and feet.

I sit up. "Don't we need to clean this up?"

"No. Natasha is doing it. I don't have enough time with you. I don't want to waste it cleaning."

I can't believe she's actually letting someone else do something for her, but I can't fault her logic. It seems that lately we just don't have enough time together.

We make our way to her SUV, and I pause.

"Babe? You'll have to drive. I can't really drive right now."

Mila glances at my knee. "Holy shit, I didn't even think of that. Are you ok right now?"

"Of course," I lie. "I just can't really push down the accelerator. Other than that, I'm fine."

I open her driver's side door for her, and she climbs in.

As I limp around the back, I take two more pills.

I'm down to twenty-two.

I chew them before I get into the truck.

When we arrive home, I stumble on the front step. My knee buckles, and almost gives out, and Mila grabs me with a gasp.

"I think maybe you should use crutches. At least until surgery."

"It's not a bad idea. The damn thing gives out whenever it wants to." Plus, it's almost impossible to bear weight… and it gets worse every day.

"I'll have Natasha stop at a drug store on her way home."

I nod. "Thanks."

She heads to peek in on Zu, who should be peacefully sleeping in her bed, and I stop in my study. I pour a glass of scotch, and as I'm drinking it, I notice the mail on my desk. I hate for it to pile up, so I sit down to look through it.

A box is on top. It's small and wrapped in brown parcel paper. There is no return address.

Intrigued, I unwrap it, and open the top.

A folded note is inside.

Keep this.

Beneath it, there is a loaded syringe of heroin.

MY PEACE

Chapter Sixteen

I shove it in my top desk drawer, trying to get it out of my sight. Just looking at the needle sends a deep craving pulsing through me. I don't know why, and it scares the fuck out of me.

But I don't have time to think on it.

Because Mila is screaming my name.

I scramble as fast I can from behind my desk, and she's bursting into my office, her eyes wild.

"Zuzu's gone, Pax. She's gone!"

"What do you mean?"

"Someone took her!"

Shock slams into me, into my gut, and Mila has a piece of paper pressed into her hand.

"What is that?" I ask and I can't feel my tongue. She thrusts it at me.

X marks the spot.

Below it, there's a phone number.

Son of a bitch. Oh my God.

I can't breathe, I can't think. I just pick up my phone and call the number.

"Hello?"

Someone answers, and I can't tell who because their voice is disguised. It's gravelly and mechanical, and it sends chills down my spine.

"Where is my daughter?" I ask abruptly.

The person laughs and they sound like a devil. "She's here. Look."

My phone vibrates in my hand, and there is a picture of Zu, asleep in the backseat of a car. She has her tiger with her.

I am relieved for one brief second. At least she is alive.

"What do you want?"

"There are a couple things," the voice tells me. "First, you cannot call the police, or she's dead. Got it?"

My heart is pulsing high in my throat and I can barely make my vocal chords work.

"Yes."

"Next, you will get on your plane, and you will fly to Angel Bay. To your home on the lake."

"Why?"

"Don't ask questions. You will go alone."

"Ok."

"Mila will not call the police. If she does, I will kill her, too. You will take the box with you. The one you just found on your desk."

I'm silent and shocked, and how did he know?

"Say yes or no."

I move my lips. "Yes."

"Good. I do believe your daughter will make it through this just fine. All you have to do is behave."

I'm silent, and I can't breathe. Mila is clinging to my arm, trying to listen, but she can't hear anything. I see the frustration and desperation in her eyes.

"Say that you're on your way. Your plane is waiting for you."

"I'm on my way."

MY PEACE

"Say that you won't call the police."

"I won't call the police. Don't hurt my daughter."

"Then behave."

The phone goes dead, and Mila is staring at me, and I stand frozen with the phone in my hand.

"What's happening?" she begs. "What's happening?"

"Leroy Ellison," I finally manage to say. "He's arranged this somehow. I have to go to Angel Bay. I think that's where they are taking her."

"Why?" Mila cries out. "I'm calling the police."

She grabs at my phone, but I don't allow it. "You can't," I tell her simply. "He'll kill you and Zuzu if you do. I have to do as he says. He has our baby, Mi."

"You can't go," she tells me firmly. "He'll kill you."

"If I don't, he'll kill Zuzu. I know he'll do it."

Mila drops into the chair, her legs unable to hold her. Her face is drained of all color. I grab her and pull her to me.

"I have to go. I will make this ok, Mila. I swear to God."

She nods and she is wordless.

"Please, rest. You have to think of the baby. Please, Mila. I'm going right now. It'll be ok. I swear it."

I kiss her hard and fast, and I grab the box out of the desk.

Then I'm out the door. There is so much adrenaline pumping through me that I don't even feel the pain in my leg as I drive Danger to the airport. I can't think, I can barely breathe. All I can think about is that picture of my daughter in the back of a stranger's car.

Her life depends on me.

I have to behave.

Just as he'd said, my plane is waiting at the airport, ready to depart. I climb the steps, and we take off within minutes.

The flight is two hours. Mila calls me and texts me several times.

"Have you heard anything?" she asks me.

"No. Please just stay inside, babe," I tell her. "Don't go out."

"Ok. Natasha is back. She has your crutches."

Mila breaks down into tears, and I console her the best I can.

"Babe, don't cry. I'll get her. It'll be ok. He wants me. Not Zuzu. It'll be ok."

"Nothing can happen to you," she cries out. "Please, Pax. God. I can't be without you. Not now."

"You won't," I tell her firmly. "Call Maddy. Have her and Gabe come over and sit with you. Set the alarm. Ok?"

"Ok," she agrees. "Please be careful."

"I will."

She hangs up, and I've never felt more alone, more scared, than I feel right now. I'm suspended above the clouds, in a plane that is flying me towards my old home, and hopefully toward my daughter.

I'm the only one who can fix this.

I know that.

When we land, I walk toward the airport and inside, there is a driver with my name on a sign.

"Sir?" he asks as I stop in front of him.

"I'm Pax Tate. Who sent you?"

He's confused. "Someone set up your transportation from the airport. Are we not needed?"

"No, you are," I tell him. "Let's go."

MY PEACE

I direct him toward Angel Bay, and within the hour, we're pulling up in front of my lake house.

He drives away, and I'm alone in front of the dark house.

I stare at it for a moment. The modern loft-style home is perched on the tip of bluffs, and I don't know what I'd expected. Perhaps that Zuzu would come running out into my arms.

But she doesn't.

All is dark.

My phone rings.

"Go inside."

"Where's my daughter?"

"Go inside."

I unlock the door, and everything is exactly like we'd left it the last time we were here. It is spotless, and without a family in it, it is lifeless.

"Go sit on the couch in front of the windows," the voice tells me. "Look out at the lake."

I look across the water, and a couple hundred yards out, there is a boat. I can see the light bobbing on the waves.

"Your daughter is out here with me."

"Prove it."

There is another photo. This time, someone's watch is in the frame, and someone's hand is holding a knife to my daughter's sleeping neck. The watch reads the current time.

"Don't hurt her," I tell them. "What do you want me to do? Do you want money?"

He laughs. "Not right now. Right now, I want you to open that box."

The syringe.

My gut tightens. "No. I'll pay you whatever you want."

"That's not what I want right now," the voice says. "Right now, I want you to take out that syringe, and pump it into your vein. All of it."

"Why?" It doesn't make any sense. Unless it is laced with something to kill me. Or perhaps to infect me with something terrible.

"It isn't for you to question me," the voice says. "I hold the cards."

"How do I know you haven't infected the needle with something?" I ask, but I'm already pulling it out. I don't have a choice. My daughter has a knife to her throat.

"You don't. Inject it."

I don't hesitate. I roll up my sleeve, and pierce my skin with the needle. The heroin floods into my blood, and I feel the sting, and the warmth, and it is all very familiar, and lord help me, it feels good. Familiar. Comforting. Warm.

"Better now?"

"Now what?" I manage to say, even though my tongue is thick, and I look around for the camera. There must be a camera here. He's watching me.

"Now, go into your bedroom. There are instructions. Leave your cellphone on the couch."

I am wooden as I enter my room, and frozen as I turn on a lamp. True to his word, there are boxes with notes on the bed. At least thirty boxes. Each note says USE ME, with a time stamped beneath it.

I open the first box. Its instructions say to use it at one am.

MY PEACE

It's a small vial of cocaine, and a mirror with a straw taped to the edge.

You've got to be fucking kidding me.

I spin around to go back out to the couch, and the door is now locked.

He's inside the house with me.

I pound on the door, but there is no answer.

I try to break it down, but it is too well made. It's reinforced because that's how I'd wanted it back when I built the house. Back when I didn't want druggies to burst in on me in my sleep, because that was the kind of company I used to keep.

I stride across the room, and find that the windows have been nailed shut from the outside.

Whoever this is, they've thought everything through.

I sit on the bed.

A video nursery monitor is on the nightstand. A note is taped to it.

Turn me on.

I do.

A grainy black and white picture pops up on the screen, of Zuzu's bedroom down the hall. She's tucked into the bed with her tiger. She's less than a hundred feet from me.

She's safe.

For now.

I breathe out, then in, then out.

She's safe.

She's in this house.

But I can't get out of this fucking room.

A paper is pushed under the door.

I pick it up.

It's 1:00. Time for your medicine.

I stare at the door.

I can't do this. What if they kill Zuzu anyway?

But what if they don't? A voice reasons with me in my head. They don't want Zuzu. They want me. It doesn't matter what happens to me as long as I keep her safe.

As long as I *behave*.

I sit on the bed, pull out the mirror, and do the line of cocaine.

MY PEACE

Chapter Seventeen

Mila

I race back to Zuzu's room to see if there are any clues there, anything at all, and there isn't. Her bed is rumpled from where her little body had been sleeping in it. Her windows are closed, and I don't know how they got into this house. It makes me feel vulnerable, out in the open, and I grab Zu's favorite blankie and inhale it.

It smells like little girl, and my eyes flood with hot tears.

She's out there, and she's alone, and she's probably crying for me. God. My stomach clenches and contracts, and I feel like throwing up.

I glance around her room, at the little tea table she'd set for tea with her teddy bears, and the castle that she'd played prince and princess in just today. I was the princess, Pax was the prince, and she was the baby who was magic.

Tears stream down my face and I can't.

I can't.

I just can't.

I reach for my phone to call Maddy, and it's not in my pocket. I'd left it in Pax's study.

Taking Zu's blanket, I rush back down the hall, and when I get there, Natasha is sitting at the desk. Her face is solemn, her hair pulled into a tight bun.

"Looking for this?" she holds up my phone.

"Yes, thank you," I reach for it, but she pulls it back.

"No. You can't have it."

I'm confused, and because I'm so addled already, it takes a minute to see the look on Natasha's face. It's cold, perfunctory, and it's not good.

She smiles, a slow grin. "Awww. You're getting it now."

"You're in on this," I saw slowly. "How…"

My voice trails off.

She smiles again.

"Let me tell you a story. Come sit down." She motions to the two chairs in front of the desk and hesitantly, I sit down. "There you go. I want to share a story with you. Will you listen?"

I don't have a choice. I nod.

"Good. There was once a girl. Let's call her Natasha, shall we? She lived a dry existence, going to college and then working as an accountant. It was so boring, so lifeless. And then, one day, she saw a story on the news. A man was convicted of killing a young mother, but it wasn't the man at all. It was her own son who did it, you see. I could see the kind look in his eyes, and I felt so sorry for him, that the justice system had failed him so miserably. What crime had he committed, really? Other than fall in love with a woman and try to show her? Her son overreacted and bumped the trigger and it was *his* fault she died. Not the kind man's. So I started writing him letters in prison."

I literally feel my eyes widen as I realize what she's saying.

"So you're… you're…"

"Shhh," she tells me, and she's looking past me, her gaze unfocused. "He's a wonderful man, Mila. He's so kind, and so forgiving. He took his admiration of Susanna a little too far, and he shouldn't have come into their house. He knows that. But that's all he did that was wrong. Pax is the one who pulled the trigger. Not Leroy."

"Pax was seven years old," I say slowly. "Leroy broke into the house with a gun, and forced Susanna to give him oral sex in front of Pax."

Natasha looks up at me sharply.

"You don't know what happened. You weren't there."

"Maybe not," I tell her. "But I was with Pax at the therapist's office when he remembered. I was with him when he remembered aloud, everything that Leroy did that day. He carved Pax's hand with an X. Did you know that? He tried to kill him, but he said he couldn't kill a kid."

"See?" Natasha is triumphant now, and her eyes have a strange light in them. "See? He can't kill a kid, because he is a kind man. He just can't do it."

"Is he the one who arranged for Zuzu to be taken?" I ask her. "Did he escape? Does he have her?"

She's disdainful now. "Of course not. He's still wrongfully imprisoned. And *I* arranged it."

She's crazy. I've always wondered about the women who wrote to inmates after they'd been imprisoned. And Natasha is crazy. She had just done a very good job of hiding it.

"How did you come to work for William?" I ask her. "Was that part of the plan?"

"Everything is part of the plan," she answers and she's proud of that. "Originally, we thought we'd hurt Pax through William, but then we saw a better way. Once Zuzu was born."

"You've been planning this for so long?" I'm breathless.

"Of course. Master-plans take time," she sniffs, as though I'm the idiot here.

"Is Zuzu all right?" I ask calmly, and I don't know how I'm remaining calm. It's like my blood is frozen as it rushes through my heart, and my daughter is out there somewhere and these people are crazy.

"Of course," she tells me. "I thought we already established that Leroy doesn't want to hurt a kid?"

"Then what are you planning on doing with her?" I ask. "She's innocent. She hasn't done a thing to anyone."

"Of course she hasn't," Natasha agrees. "She's fine. And she will stay fine as long as Pax does what we ask."

"And what are you asking of him?" I ask. My hands shake against the arms of the chair.

Natasha smiles.

"Only for his life. That's not too much, is it?"

MY PEACE

Chapter Eighteen
Pax

Light shines in from the bedroom windows, and I stare at it for a second. The sun rays filter through the air, and the dust motes spiral and I reach out a hand to touch them.

I haven't slept all night.

Doing four lines of coke will do that to a person. I doubt I'll sleep for days.

Through the monitor, I hear my daughter singing, through my closed door and hers, and I relax my tight muscles. She's still here. She's still alive, and thankfully, from the sounds of it, she doesn't know the danger she's in.

Thank God.

I straighten my leg and adjust my back.

I'm sitting on the floor, pressed to the wall, and it is holding me up. The coolness of it bleeds into my skin, and I soak it up. I concentrate on it, because it grounds me in this moment, and keeps everything real.

Temperature is real.

The wall is real.

Focus on what is real, I tell myself. *Zuzu is real. Mila is real.*

Mila. *God.* She's probably so worried. I heard my phone ring numerous times, and then I think it was turned off. I haven't heard it from hours, and I know Mila wouldn't just stop calling. Not if she was able.

Lord, the thought of her being *unable* turns my blood cold.

But that's not happening, I tell myself. They don't want her. They want me.

A paper is slipped beneath the door.

I open it. *It's time.*

I stare at the boxes. I don't feel the pain in my leg anymore. The drugs have definitely dulled all of my senses. The idea that I used to live like this… it's so foreign to me. It's like living through a fog, not really living at all.

I open the box, and am surprised to see clear capsules filled with white powder. I don't know what they are. PCP, maybe? I don't bother worrying about it.

I swallow them.

Within minutes, I'm swearing, and my vision is blurred. Definitely PCP. My skin starts crawling, there are ants on it, and I fight the urge to scratch them.

It's a side-effect, and there are no ants. I know that.

Yet, at the minutes tick past, it's hard to know anything.

Everything becomes subjective. Everything is a gray area. Even the sounds of my daughter fade away and I can't focus on her anymore. I've got enough drugs pumping through my veins that I can't even see her face or my wife's, even when I try to imagine them in my head.

Leroy is good at this. He's planned out exactly how much drugs he can force me to take without me dying. He's dragging it out, loading me up, then bringing me back down with heroin.

He wants to make me suffer.

Out of the corner of my eye, I see things. I see movements, and shadows, all moving along the walls and

MY PEACE

while I know they aren't really there, I can't help but check. I'm losing it.

I know I'm losing it.

Before I'm completely gone, I try to break the door down one last time. I'm a strong guy. I know that. I don't make a dent in the door. I think it's been reinforced from the outside somehow.

I try to break the windows.

They don't budge. They've been replaced with shatter-proof glass. He's thought of everything.

Son of a bitch.

I slump to the floor. I'm not giving up.

I look at the video monitor.

Zuzu is playing by herself, combing the hair on one of her dolls. Her door is closed, and I'm sure it's locked, and I wonder what they've told her about her parents? Did they tell her we'd be there soon?

I shout through the door.

"Zuzu! Sweetheart! I'll be there soon. Don't be afraid."

She doesn't even look up. She can't hear me.

I examine the door again, and now that I'm really looking at it, I see it's not the same door I had installed. I think this one might be soundproof.

It must be. As a test, I bang on it as hard as I can.

Zuzu doesn't look up. She can't hear me.

No one can hear me.

My scalp buzzes, and I tug at my hair, and then I force my hand to still. It's the PCP. It's the PCP making me crazy. I've got to stop.

I force myself to sit on the floor again, and I pick a spot on the wall, and I stare at it, forcing my breath to be even. In, then out. In, then out. One, two. One, two. I focus on the pattern. I focus on my heart beat. I focus on making my breath fill my lungs up like a balloon, then forcing it all out, like the balloon is deflating.

If I do this, if I keep my mind active, and focused, I won't lose it. It will be tethered to me.

It will still be mine.

Leroy can't take that.

Not if I don't allow it.

I glance out the windows for a moment, and the waves are crashing outside, and I realize something.

I can't hear them.

MY PEACE

Chapter Nineteen

Mila

I'm in my room without a phone.

Natasha took it, and Natasha has a gun, and has she always had a gun in this house? It must've been hidden in her bedroom and I didn't even know it.

I should've listened to my instincts about her. I knew something was off. I just thought she was after my husband.

And I guess she was, just not in the way I thought.

I pace. The door is locked, and I have no means of communication. I'm sure Natasha is answering my texts from Maddy as though she is me, and no one will ever know that I'm being locked up in here. I'm going to be here forever, or until they decide what to do with me.

There is a knock, then the key is turned, and the door is opened.

Natasha walks in with a tray.

"Here."

She puts it on the bed, and picks up the TV remote. "I've got something for you."

She messes with the television, and then a black and white picture comes up. A surveillance video. It's not high-definition, certainly, but it's clear enough.

It's Pax.

I suck in a breath, and my husband is sprawled on the floor in a room.

Looking closer, I decide it's our bedroom in Angel Bay. There are small boxes on the bed, the size of jewelry boxes. Some are neatly stacked, and some are open in a pile.

Pax isn't moving.

"Is he ok?" I ask quickly. Natasha stares at me.

"You can see for yourself."

Pax is staring at nothing, his eyes open, and is he alive?

God, is he alive? My heart pounds and pounds, threatening to leap from my chest.

I touch the screen, his hand, and he's not moving. There's no signs of blood or a struggle. His legs are long, his body is taut, and he's not moving.

"Come on, baby," I tell him. "Please be alive."

Natasha laughs and I shove her away from me.

She backhands me across the face, and my head snaps around. I taste blood in my mouth, and my cheek is on fire, and I rush at her, my blood boiling and red blurring my vision.

But then there is something cold and metal in my side.

She brought her gun.

Fuck.

I back off.

"Is he alive?" I ask her coldly.

She grins.

"Eat. You need to for the baby."

"As if you care."

"You should put a cool cloth on that," she suggests, gesturing at my mouth, and then she's gone again. I ignore my swelling lip, and instead focus on my husband again.

Is his hand in a different place? Did he move while I wasn't looking?

I sink to my knees.

MY PEACE

"Please, please please," I beg. I'm not sure if I'm begging God or Pax.

I'm frozen in place and he doesn't move.

"Please, God," I mumble, without taking my eyes off the screen.

He's so completely still.

I wait. I ignore the food tray and I watch my husband for any sign of life. For anything.

He gives me nothing.

For an hour, for sixty long, frustrating minutes, I stare at him, and he doesn't move. But then... then...

Something is slipped under the door of his room.

I peer at it.

It looks like a folded piece of paper.

Pax blinks.

He blinked.

The knowledge rams into me and I cry from relief. He's not dead.

He's not dead.

Slowly, slowly, slowly, he reaches over and takes the paper. He unfolds it. He reads it.

He gets to his feet.

He grabs a box.

He takes a syringe out. He taps the barrel, he flicks at his arm.

"No," I breathe. "No. Pax, don't!"

He plunges it into his arm without blinking again. He stares at the wall, like a robot or a machine, and he doesn't blink. I don't think he's feeling a thing. His eyes are wide open.

When he's finished, he puts it back in the box, and tosses it in a pile of empties. There are so many empty boxes, and had they all contained drugs?

I'm stunned. I'm numb.

What the hell is happening?

Why is this happening?

Pax sits back down on the floor in the same place he'd been. He resumes staring at the wall, his eyes wide open and unblinking.

My chest quivers, my hands shake.

He's not fighting?

This isn't like him.

I scan his surroundings. It's definitely our bedroom. It's our bed, our night-tables. My gaze stops on the night-table. The nursery monitor is there, and the screen is on.

Something… something looks like it's moving. But I can't see it clearly enough. It almost looks like the outline of a small person. Maybe a child.

Is it Zuzu?

Please, God, I pray again. Please. I'll give you anything. Take my life, not theirs.

I sink to the floor and watch the screen.

It's the only thing I can do.

MY PEACE

Chapter Twenty

Pax

Time has no meaning now.

At some points, it passes slowly, and at others, it passes quickly. It all depends on what is in the box.

This time, it is cocaine. For the fourth time today.

He has planned the exact drugs that will counter each other out throughout the day… some speed me up, some slow me down. They're carefully planned to keep me alive. To keep me going. To keep me suffering.

"Is Mila alive?" I ask when a note is shoved under the door.

There is no answer. I doubt they can hear me.

This note also tells me to look in the top dresser drawer.

Two boxes of granola bars and a dozen bottles of water are there. I ignore them. I'm not hungry. My heart is racing though. The cocaine speeds it up and I'm flying and I'm numb, and all of my emotions are dulled like I'm sinking in a murky pond.

I'm worried about Zuzu and Mila, I know that I am, but at the moment, I don't actually feel it. I don't feel the emotions that should accompany my thoughts. They're gone. Leroy has taken them from me. In theory and in practice. In reality and in my head.

I glance at the nursery monitor.

Zuzu is sleeping. She's safe on the bed, and she's sleeping.

I can't save her.

They are going to kill me here. I know they are. I want to look inside all of the boxes, but at the same time, I don't want to know just yet how they've planned my end.

Will it be a fatal dose of heroin?

Will it be too much cocaine?

Maybe they'll make me drink antifreeze.

It's hard to say.

All I know is, at the moment, I don't care.

Every ounce of my caring is gone. It's been taken.

The longer I take these drugs, the more I will feel empty. I know that from experience.

The walls start to close in on me, and my skin starts to itch, and the ceiling seems to fall. I focus harder on the wall in front of me. If I don't, I will lose my mind, and he can't have that. He can take my feelings, but he can't have my mind.

My thoughts are my own.

I breathe in and out, I focus hard, harder, harder.

I picture Zuzu and Mila. I know I love them. I know I do. Love is a fact. It isn't always a feeling. I don't need to feel it at the moment to know it's true.

I picture Zu's blonde curls and bright eyes, her bright smile and her tiny fingers. She holds my hand at every opportunity. I imagine walking across the garden with her, playing hide and seek, which Mila watches. Mila's eyes are clear too, and her smile is like the sun. She watches us, and the love she feels is in her eyes, and she reaches for me, and my stomach clenches.

They're going to kill me, and that will kill Mila. It will kill her.

I don't care for myself, but I care what it will do to her.

MY PEACE

She's been through so much already. She shouldn't have to go through this, too.

I stand up, and because I know they are watching me through the small camera in the corner, I take the remaining boxes and throw them as hard as I can against the wall. I stomp on them. Then I flip off the camera.

The tiny red light blinks and I know they see.

I stare at them without blinking.

"Fuck you," I tell them.

The light blinks.

They see me.

I smile.

***

Mila

Pax rages against captivity.

His muscles bulge as he throws the boxes of drugs against the wall and then stomps them into oblivion. When they are tattered and torn and flat, he flips off the camera, and they must be watching him through it. I smile because this is my husband. This is the man I married.

He won't take it lying down.

I'm terrified about what they will do to our daughter, but I know that they will do what they're going to do regardless. It was never contingent upon what Pax does. I know that.

The door bursts open and two men dressed in black storm in. They fight with Pax, and the movement seems to be slightly delayed. Every few seconds, it catches up, and it seems like it skipped a frame.

One is kicking him now, over and over in his gut. My husband's body jerks and lifts with each blow. I call out and scream, but they don't stop. I can feel each blow as if they are doing it to me. That is how closely my husband and I are connected.

When he is limp, I'm limp.

My brow is sweaty, my hands are shaking.

He is no longer conscious, and they heft him onto the bed, restraining him there. His hands and feet are bound and he is bound to the bed itself. He isn't going anywhere. His face bleeds, his nose looks broken.

His head lolls to the side and they leave him there, alone and broken.

"Pax," I murmur. "Please…"

I cry into my hands, and I am so helpless. He's dying in a room alone, and I can't get to him, and I can't help.

I'm taking a shaky breath when he finally moves.

He turns his head and stares at the camera.

He smiles and his teeth are red.

MY PEACE

Chapter Twenty-One

Pax

I drift in and out of consciousness.

I can't move. Not really.

The bindings bite into my hands and my ankles, but I don't feel it. I don't feel my knee. I don't feel anything. I don't even feel my face, and I know it must be ragged. They kicked the the shit out of me.

I feel nothing.

The light fades in and out with my consciousness, day turns into night.

I can't turn my head far enough to see the nursery monitor anymore, so I can't see Zuzu. I can't check on her, I have no idea what she's doing.

"Let her go," I ask them when they come back in later to inject me. "Let her go. I'm here now. He wanted me. He has me."

They don't say anything. Their faces are covered with black ski masks, and I don't know why they've bothered with that. They aren't letting me live. I know that.

I try to think of my options.

I don't have any.

All I have is money.

"I can pay you," I tell them the next time they come. "I can pay you more than he can."

They don't say a thing. They inject me, the room swirls, and I'm out like a light.

I don't wake up for what must be hours. My body is stiff when I awaken, but there is no pain. I guess I should be thankful for that smallest of favors.

I try to focus.

What should a person do when they are a bound captive?

What can I do?

I examine the room again. Nothing has changed.

I know there are at least two of them.

I know they have what seems to be an unlimited supply of drugs.

I know they were prepared.

I focus on staying conscious, and it is actually difficult. My body is fighting back against all of the toxins in my system. It wants to sleep them off, to regain strength during slumber. I can't do that.

I have to think.

Think, think, think.

I have to stay calm.

They come back.

One of them speaks.

"We were told you'd want to know what your mother said about you."

I focus on that, on my mother. She was kind and warm. And Leroy said… that he had something to tell me. Something she'd said.

I remember now.

I wait.

The guy laughs, and his lips are dry. I can only see his eyes and lips through the holes in the mask. His eyes are

MY PEACE

brown. Dull brown. His lips are chapped, flaky in the corners.

"I'm not going to tell you. Not while you are resisting like this. You were told to behave. You aren't."

He places a lock of blond hair on my chest. The curl of it gleams in the sun from the windows. It's Zuzu's.

I struggle to turn, to see the monitor.

"Don't you touch her," I shout at him.

He laughs again.

"She's fine," he tells me finally. "For now."

My head falls back against the bed. My wrists are bleeding from the binding.

"You can only behave if you do it on your own accord," he continues. "It doesn't count if we have to force you. Are you ready to behave?"

I nod.

"Are you sure?" he asks sternly.

I nod.

"Fine. We're going to untie you. And you're going to do as you're told, or the next thing I bring you won't be your daughter's hair."

I nod again, and when they untie me, the blood flows back into my limbs in a flood of pins and needles.

"Son of a bitch," I mutter before I can stop myself, as I rub at my hands and feet.

The guy laughs. The other doesn't say much.

I slump into the bed. They bring in fresh boxes, crisp white cardboard, filled with poisons. I flinch. The second guy thrusts one into my hands.

"It's time," he says, and it's the first time I've heard his voice. I don't recognize it.

They leave me unbound with the box in my lap.

I look inside.

With a sigh, I snort the coke. Once again, my heart-rate speeds up and pounds and pumps and I'm afraid it might explode.

It doesn't.

MY PEACE

Chapter Twenty-Two

Mila

I hate Natasha.

I hate looking at her. I hate smelling her cloying honeysuckle perfume.

"Why are you wearing that scent?" I demand. "Because Leroy likes it, or to make Pax feel comfortable around you? I know that Susanna used to wear it. I remember Pax telling me so."

She smiles.

"Pax does enjoy it." She smirking now, baiting me.

"You wear too much of it," I tell her. "I shouldn't be able to smell it from across the room."

"Your husband didn't have to smell it from a distance," she tells me, her eyes narrowed. "He liked to bury his nose in my neck and smell it up close."

"No, he didn't."

She laughs, and she's mocking me.

"You seem awfully sure of yourself," she says finally, and she sits in the chair next to my bed. I wasn't kidding, she *is* wearing too much perfume, and it actually gives me a headache. I rub at my temples.

"Of course I'm sure of myself," I answer tiredly. "Pax doesn't want you. I know that."

Even still, the memory of him emerging from the garage with her, in the middle of the night, it haunts me.

When I least expect it, it has popped into my head and tormented me.

"He does, though," Natasha says, playing to my doubt. "I saw it in his eyes. The way he touched me that night in the garage. He wasn't just leaning on me for support, he was feeling me, Mila. He was feeling my body. He wanted me."

My stomach clenches, and I force myself to relax. She's lying to upset me.

Don't rise to the bait.

"I gave him muscle relaxers," she adds. "I was able to comfort him, to soothe him, in a time when he didn't trust you enough to tell you about his pain."

That startles me.

"What muscle relaxers?"

Pax wouldn't do that. He wouldn't take something so strong. He wouldn't tempt himself.

"He didn't tell you?" Natasha feigns innocence now. "I'm surprised. I thought he told you everything."

I'm silent now. Whatever Pax has done, he did it to protect me from something. I know my husband well enough to know that.

"Little did he know, though," Natasha says casually as she bites into an apple. It crunches loudly. "That I laced those pills."

This snaps my head up.

"With what?" I try to stay calm, but my heart is racing. "What did you lace them with?"

She takes another bite.

"With methamphetamines."

She shrugs like it's no big deal.

MY PEACE

My heart seems to stop, as I think about the recent past, about Pax's mood swings, and his abnormal behavior. I swallow hard.

It all makes sense.

So much sense.

"But why?" I ask.

"Why not?" she shrugs again, and I want to slap her head off her shoulders. "Because it's fun being the cat. Pax is the mouse," she adds unnecessarily.

"You were fucking with him," I say.

"You're a bright one."

"Fuck you."

"Such words coming out of a lady's mouth," she chuckles. "I wanted to make him pay. What's the best way to make someone like him pay? He had a rough childhood. He finally had a life that he enjoys. The only way to pay is take all of that away."

I feel a twinge in my belly. I've got to calm down. The pain is sharp, and I press my hand to it.

"Get out," I spit. "Get the fuck out."

"You don't get to tell me what to do," she mentions. "But I don't like you any more than you like me." She stands up, and tosses her apple core into my trash, then slowly and deliberately, walks out. I have another sharp pain.

I rush to the bathroom and yank down my pants.

There is blood in my underwear.

Chapter Twenty-Four

Pax

I wake craving coke.

I crave the sting in my nose and the rush in my blood and the numbness in my mouth.

It's something that slams me into reality hard, like a truckload full of stones.

I'm addicted to cocaine now. And heroin. And probably PCP. They've made sure of that. And for what? What is the point?

How did they manage to get me addicted within two weeks?

I'm an addict.

It happened so fast.

I feel empty inside, something that begins in my belly, flows through my veins, and ends in my heart. It doesn't matter what they do to me now. They've done the worst they can do.

I promised Mila years ago that I'd never hurt her again. This will kill her, and *that* will kill me.

I sit staunchly on the floor, waiting as they come in. I don't know what they're doing, and I don't care.

"You've been a good boy today," the man says, the one who always talks. "So we've brought you a reward."

MY PEACE

He hands me a piece of paper. It looks like it's been ripped out of something, and I decide it's a journal page.

It's yellowed with age, and it's written in faded blue ink pen in a masculine scrawl. It's Leroy Ellison's journal.

One page.

Today, I watched the house for an hour before I crept to the window and looked in. The father isn't home from work yet. He neglects them terribly. Always gone, comes home late. He's addicted to work, I think. The boy is rambunctious. He's always into something, and she chases behind him. Wherever he goes, she follows. I'm not sure that I would want him to come after I take her. We shall see.

She's a good mother, though. I admire that about her. If I don't take him, she'd resent me. I don't want that. It's a quandary.

Jesus.

My breath leaves my body as I read the words.

He'd observed our home for quite some time before he'd broken in and forced himself on my mother. God only knows for how long.

She's a good mother, though.

Those words, even though they're from a psychopath, warm my numb heart. Even a psychopath could see her love for me. He doesn't have feelings. Yet he recognized hers. That's how strong they were.

She loved me so much she died protecting me.

It's something I thought I'd dealt with, but the magnitude of that overwhelms me now. If it hadn't been for me, if I hadn't rushed out of that closet to "save" her, she'd still be alive. She'd still be smiling. She'd still be here.

But she's not.
And it's my fault.
I swallow hard. Then I get up, cross the room, and open the next box two hours earlier than I am supposed. I inject the heroin.

The pain disappears.

Hazy warm comfort replaces it.

The blackness, the void, it sucks me in. There is no pain in the abyss.

It doesn't last long enough though, for barely an hour. So I open the next box early, too. It's also heroine. I'm thankful for that. I press the plunger and close my eyes.

The pain, the emotion, the consciousness, all disappear into nothing.

I close my eyes.

***

I open my eyes.

I blink. My eyes are dry so I blink again. Then again.

I am flat on my back, I think.

I must be, because I think I'm staring at a ceiling. There's a light above me. It comes in and then out of focus.

It's hard to say, because I feel like I'm floating. Through space, through water, through something. Something murky, yet I can't touch it. I stretch out a hand. It comes back with nothing. Just air.

I'm the perfect temperature. Not hot, not cold.

There is no pain. That's the most blessed thing. My leg doesn't hurt. My ribs don't hurt. My heart doesn't hurt. Not anymore.

MY PEACE

Nothing bothers me here, not in this abyss. Worries, stress, reality. All are gone. Far from me, far from here.

I can't feel.

I can't think.

I don't need to.

Still, even though it's perfect here, and black and void, something isn't right. I know that. It niggles at me, bothering me, like an itch. I scratch at it, at the thought, and I realize that it bothers me because I shouldn't be here.

This is an old familiar place, a place I haven't visited in a long time.

Oblivion.

How did I get here?

What the fuck happened?

I furrow my brow and try to think…

My brain is foggy. It takes me a few minutes, then a few minutes more, to remember.

I'm in my bedroom. Mila isn't here.

But drugs are. That's what I need right now. It's driving me. The urge to inhale, to burn.

I want to burn.

I open a box.

Chapter Twenty-Five

The boy is easy.

Today, I called him over to the mail truck and gave him two pieces of candy, and asked where his mother was. She was in the kitchen making lemonade.

The boy took me in, and I hand delivered her mail.

She was surprised, but pleasantly so. She said she'd never had anyone take the trouble. She gave me a glass of lemonade, and we went outside and sat in the shade while the boy kicked a ball on the lawn.

I could live like this.

I can tolerate the boy.

The woman's name is Susanna, and it suits her. She is like a blue sky and sunny day, and she smells like sweet honeysuckle.

I imagined that I was licking her skin today, and I must've lost myself in the fantasy. She noticed, and asked if I was ok.

I had to excuse myself.

I beat off in the mail-truck thinking about her.

Soon, soon. It will be her.

The journal entry makes me sick to my stomach.

I let him into our home? I was swayed by two pieces of candy? God.

MY PEACE

She welcomed him, and gave him lemonade and a rest from his weary day, and he repaid her by assaulting her later. What kind of monster is he?

The outrage that I know I feel is dulled by the drugs.

I know it is there, lurking in my heart, though.

My anger is a slumbering beast. It has always been there, hidden from the world. I masked it, but I couldn't exorcise it.

It is a part of me.

I know that now.

I sit on the floor, and I grab a box.

I'm three boxes ahead of schedule, and my captors like that. In fact, they rewarded me today with the journal page. I'm sure they'll continue.

The higher I get, the more pages they'll give me.

The drugs dull the pain. It's a win-win situation.

I shoot up, and the familiar burn tears into me, spreading through my arm like a raging fire. I drop my head back, and I sit in the window seat, and I stare out at the lake.

It makes me feel small. It is vast and wide, and it could suck me in and drown me.

In this moment, I almost wish it would.

It would suck away all of this.

There would be no more worry, no more fear.

I close my eyes. I know this is the heroin talking. But more and more, it's getting harder to tell the difference.

***

When I wake, there is another journal page in my lap.

They'd been in here, and I hadn't even woke.

I blink my eyes, then blink them harder, trying to focus.

I'm fucked up.

More fucked up than I've ever been.

It's their point, I guess.

I look at the computer monitor.

Zuzu is sitting on her bed, and she's crying. I have her golden curl in my pocket, and I grasp it. She must be lonely. She must be wondering where her mother and I are.

"I'm here," I tell her, although I know she can't hear. "I'm here."

She still cries, and I'm still alone.

I slump into the seat. I read the paper.

Tomorrow is the day.
Everything is planned.
I will tell Susanna how I feel about her, and she will be so grateful that I have come to save her. We will go live in my father's cabin in the country. No one knows where it is, and Susanna can teach the boy herself. There will be no need for school. I don't want any questions raised. I have thought of everything.
Our life will be grand.
She will be grateful.

He mentioned grateful twice.

He was definitely delusional. He thought he was rescuing my mother from a bad life. It would be laughable if it hadn't ended so tragically.

She thought she was being kind to a loner.

And he *was* a loner.

But he was also crazy. We just hadn't known it.

MY PEACE

It makes me wonder how many people I've come into contact with in my life who have secretly been insane or twisted.

It's amazing what can lie beneath a false demeanor.

Everyone has a façade, I guess.

My façade was that I'm not an addict.

I lied to myself and I lied to everyone else.

To be fair, I thought I wasn't. But it was always there, under the surface, waiting to re-emerge.

Leroy might've forced my hand, but this is all me.

I'm pathetic.

I grab a box because what is the point of doing anything else now?

I'm going to die.

I'm an addict.

So I'm going to do what addicts do.

I use.

It's cocaine this time.

I snort one line, then another.

I grab another box.

It doesn't matter anymore. When they kill me, I won't even notice.

I push the plunger of heroin into my arm.

The room swirls into a binge of bright colors, too much to fathom, too much to sustain. I close my eyes against the brightness, against the dizziness, and I swirl in and among them, a vague hue in a vibrant rainbow. I'm only a piece of this fabric, only a strand.

I'm unraveling, too.

I'm full of holes.

***

They are pleased with me.

They've had to replace the boxes.

I used all of the others, and left them in a pile on the bed.

The man smiles as he re-enters the room, his arms full of white cardboard.

"I have treats for you," he says, and he pus them down. "This is the last of them. Here is this, too."

He hands me another page of the journal.

I glance at it, but my drive is gone. I can't feel. I'm empty. I'm a void.

"That's the last of the boxes?" I ask woodenly. He nods. "What happens when they're gone?"

He shrugs. "Let's worry about that when you get to the last box, shall we?"

I rifle through them, hunting. He laughs.

"It's not there. I'll bring it in separately when the time comes."

It won't take me long to go through these. Maybe a day. Two days at the most. It doesn't matter. Nothing does.

"Send Zuzu home," I tell him and my voice is dead. It lacks all emotion. "I've earned it."

"You haven't yet," he says. "But you will."

I look away. He leaves.

I read the journal page.

I'm sitting outside of the house.

The husband isn't home yet, as I knew he wouldn't be. He never is. I won't even bother killing him. He'll barely notice they're gone. I saw them eating through the window.

MY PEACE

Macaroni and cheese and salad. I heard the boy say it's his favorite. He'll have to learn to like things like venison and rabbit after we leave. The next time I write in this journal, they will be with me. My life will be whole, and so will theirs.

I think back to that night.

I'd been in bed. I'd heard something in my mother's room. I'd gotten out of bed, and padded down the hall, stepping over a toy on my way. A dump truck.

She was in there, and she was begging for my life.

Please don't hurt him, she'd begged. She was crying and I'd never heard her cry before. Her nose was bleeding and it was spattered on her shirt. Leroy had a gun.

"Run, Pax," she'd screamed at me, but Leroy grabbed me. He'd told me to make my mom behave. *Can you help your mommy be a good girl?*

I swallow now, and acidic bile is in my throat. It burns as it slides back down.

I'll do anything. Please don't hurt him!

Anything? He'd asked, and his teeth were yellow.

He unbuttoned his pants and they dropped to the floor. He had a coiled snake tattoo on his hip.

Don't tread on me.

My mom hadn't wanted me to see, so Leroy had shoved me into the closet, but I could still see through the slats.

He shoved her down in front of him, grabbing her by the hair.

If you don't do this, I'll kill your son as you watch.

For so long, I had blocked these memories out of my head, but I can see them now. As if they'd happened yesterday. I can't un-see them. I can't shake them.

I was overcome with wanting to help her. Her shoulders were shaking and she was helpless, and I was the only one who could.

So I'd rushed out and tried.

And she'd died.

Trying to help her had killed her.

I won't make that same mistake again.

I watch Zuzu on the monitor. She's still now. She probably cried herself to sleep.

I can't fight them, or she'll die.

I can't risk it.

I open another box.

I push the plunger down, and the heroin disappears into my vein. My consciousness goes with it.

This is for the best.

MY PEACE

Chapter Twenty-Six

Mila

I've been in this bedroom for eight days. I have bled a little, off an on, but I try to keep my anxiety at a minimum, and I try to lay still in bed.

The only thing I can see is Pax on the monitor, but at least he's untied now. That's something. And he's alive.

That's everything.

He sits on the floor now, staring at the wall, and then abruptly, he climbs up and does push-ups. I lose track of how many. He moves fast, like a machine. I don't know why he's so frenzied and focused.

The doorbell rings. I can hear it vaguely from through the house. It rang once the other day, too. I have no idea who it was since I can't see from this room. All I have here is a view of the gardens and the pool. Once, I thought it was charming and quiet. Today, it secludes and isolates me.

I did finally eat. I had to for the baby. I drank my water and ate my toast, and I cup my belly protectively now. While my baby is here, inside of my body, they can't take it like they took Zuzu.

Children make you vulnerable. That is certainly true. They ripped my heart out when they took her.

I can't think of her right now. Because if I do, I'll lose my mind.

I put my hand on Pax's on the television screen. He's still now, quiet. Sweat beads on his brow.

Anyone on the outside looking in would think that we have the world on a string, but here we are... separated by a thousand miles and two locks rooms....against our will.

He's there.

I'm here.

I take a breath, and steel myself.

There has to be something I can do.

I pace, then pace more.

And then... then... there's a movement. Out of the corner of my eye.

I turn, and there is someone outside my window. Hunched down, but I still see them. Gasping, I cross the room and peer out, and Roger is peering back at me.

Pax's driver.

His eyes are wide.

I'm sure mine are too.

"Are you ok?" he mouths. I shake my head no.

He nods in confirmation.

"What are you doing?"

Natasha's voice comes from the doorway. I turn quickly, trying to block Roger.

"Staring outside. It's all I can do. You've taken everything else."

She smiles, and brings in a sandwich along with a bottle of water. "That's true, isn't it?" she agrees. "You only have what we give you at this point."

My phone is in her pocket. I see the corner of it sticking out. I try to ponder a way to get it, but with Roger right outside, I don't take the chance.

MY PEACE

I sit on the bed so that her attention is on me, rather than the window.

"When are you going to let me go?" I ask her.

"Not until after I'm long gone," she says pleasantly. I get the feeling she's determined to not lose her cool with me again.

"What about my husband?"

She levels her gaze at me, and it is cold. "I think we already established that."

Ice forms over my heart and shivers run down my spine. There isn't much time left. I feel it.

I count the minutes until she leaves the room, and then I scurry across the room to my nightstand. There is a sketchpad inside, and a piece of charcoal for drawing. It's not the best to write with, but it has to work.

I scrawl out a message.

Held captive. They have Pax at the lakehouse. Call my sister and tell her. We're not supposed to call the police. They have Zuzu.

I race back to the window, where Roger is waiting, hunched down.

He reads my words and his eyes widen in alarm. I nod.

Hurry, I mouth silently. I flip the page over and scribble one last thing.

They're going to kill Pax.

He spins around and is gone, hugging the side of the house as he goes. My heart is racing and my hands are clammy. Our lives are literally in the hands of someone else, a car driver that Pax hadn't even wanted.

I try to focus. I try to sit still, but I can't. My fingers shake, my toes. My mouth is dry, my thoughts are blurry. I have too much adrenaline and no way to use it.

So I get up and pace. I do circles around the room, and I feel like I'm going to hyperventilate. I breathe in, then out.

I don't know what is going to happen, but I had to do something.

It was never going to end well.

At least this way, we'll go down fighting.

Even if we all die.

Zuzu's face flashes in front of me, and even though they've been using her to keep me docile, I know they'll kill her too. They won't have a choice. They'll have to get rid of us all.

But Roger knows now.

He'll tell Maddy and Gabe, and they'll help us.

Gabe was an Army Ranger. He'll know what to do.

He has to.

MY PEACE

Chapter Twenty-Seven

Pax

"You have a call," the man tells me, bringing my phone into the room.

I stare at the phone in confusion.

"It's him," he adds.

Him.

Leroy.

I reach out my hand.

"What?"

"What a nice greeting for your old friend. I hope you've been enjoying your time there."

I'm silent.

The room is spinning, and I'm not quite sure if my head is sitting straight on my neck.

"Keep going," he encourages me. "Once you get to the end, once you finish all the boxes, you will achieve two things. First, Zuzu will be sent back to her mother. Second, I will tell you what you want to know. Your mother's last words. Keep going."

The line goes dead.

He clearly didn't want me to say anything incriminating on the recorded prison line. He took quite a chance to get me on the phone at all. He must've thought I was too doped up to focus.

That's partially true.

I do pushups to pump the drugs through my veins faster.

I need to work it though my system so that I can get to the end.

I have to finish.

I have to save my daughter, and I have to hear my mother's last words.

I don't know why I want to hear them.

I just do.

It's a need at this point, as real to me as my need for heroin.

Slowly, methodically, throughout the day, I work my way through the boxes.

One

By

One

By

One.

I am focused on that.

No matter how the room spins, or the blackness threatens to overtake me, I continue.

I lost consciousness

Once

Twice

Three times.

When I wake, it is night.

Early evening, I think. The light is dying on the lake, in oranges and golds and ambers. I stare at it, watching it flit to and fro, and I put my hand on the window.

I loved this place once. I loved the views of the lake and the seclusion.

MY PEACE

I can feel Mila here, even still. One of her pictures hangs on the wall, a breathtaking painting of the sun. It is an explosion of abstract vision, and I wish I was in the canvas, and away from here.

But I'm not.

And I only have a short way left to go.

I reach for the last box.

If I finish this, they'll bring me the very last one.

It will be over.

I will have won.

Even if I die, I won.

Chapter Twenty-Eight

Mila

It's been twelve hours since Roger left.

The minutes have ticked past slowly. Natasha brought me a dinner tray, and it was all I could do to act normally.

Surely, something will happen soon.

Did Roger believe me?

Maybe he misunderstood.

It's easy to be paranoid when I'm here alone.

Every sound lifts my head.

Every time, it's nothing.

Every time, I'm crushed.

I pray. I pace. I pray. I pace.

Nothing happens.

I shower, I go to bed.

It's the middle of the night before I hear something.

Something distant, something in the house.

It's not a screech, it's more of a crash.

A loud one.

I lunge from the bed for the first time in days. My legs are weak, and they almost give out, but I make it to the door, and I bang on it, screaming.

Through it, I hear a commotion. Scuffling, yelling, a loud shot. A shot?

Then,

MY PEACE

It's quiet.
Then.
Then.
"M'am, stand away from the door."

It's a man's voice, assertive and loud. I step away, scurrying to the bed, and my door comes splintering in, loudly and forcibly, and the pieces fall onto the floor. Everything next happens in a blur.

People surround me.
Everything is buzzing.
My heart pounds.
There are so many people. Police, EMTs.

"Where is my daughter?" I ask someone. They are taking my blood pressure, taking my vitals, wrapping a blanket around my shoulders. My teeth are chattering, and I didn't even realize it.

"We don't know yet," the EMT says. "Don't worry, m'am."

"And my husband? What about Pax?" I demand, and my voice is loud, and I might be screaming.

"We don't know anything yet," someone else says.

"Is he alive?" I ask, and I'm scared, terrified. I yank away from the EMTs.

"I don't know yet, m'am," she says again. It's easy for her to be calm, because it's not her life, her family, that we're talking about.

I break away and run from the bedroom, and there is a body covered by a sheet in the living room. A giant bloodstain seeps into the floor, and through the sheet, and oh my God, that is Natasha. I know it. She'd dead. I know that, too.

I pause in my tracks, and my hand is over my mouth and my breath is in my throat, and then…

Then…

"Mila?"

My sister is rushing toward me in a jacket and she smells like the cold outdoors. She grabs me tight, scooping me into a hug.

"Oh, my god," she moans into my hair as she rocks me to and fro. "Oh my God. You're safe now. You're safe."

"What about Pax?" I say simply, and she pulls away and looks at me.

"I don't know yet."

MY PEACE

Chapter Twenty-Nine

Pax

I've used everything.

Everything is empty.

The boxes, my heart, my soul. All of it.

I am a vessel and I have been used up. Depleted.

Now, all I can do is wait.

I am sprawled on the bed, and I'm not sitting, or lying. I'm halfway in between. I don't have the balance to do one or the other.

I am flailing in time, in the moment. I am existing, and not much more.

I am only waiting.

For the end.

For the last thing.

It is night.

I will die at night.

It's fitting, I decide, as the door opens and the moonlight shines in on the floor. I will die in oblivion. It's where I belong, anyway.

"You have done well," the man tells me as he eyes the empty pile of cardboard. He has the last one in his hands. "Are you ready to finish?"

I nod, because I am. When I am gone, nothing can hurt Mila again. She can take Zuzu and start anew somewhere, with someone who isn't fucked up like me. I will save them by doing this.

"This is how it will work," the man says, and he sets the box next to me. "Everything you need is in that box, including the last journal page. It will tell you what you've been wanting to know. After you've read it, you will finish it. Once it is done, I will take your daughter back to your wife. They will live happily ever after. Do you have any questions?"

"How do I know you will stick to your word?" I ask and my words are sluggish and slurred from the drugs.

"You don't," he says directly. "But I will. I have nothing against you personally. I'm paid to do a job. That is all."

I nod.

"Anything else?"

I think on that. "I want to leave a note for my wife."

"No. That's not possible."

"Will you send a message to her?" I ask. "Will you tell her that I love her?"

"If she doesn't already know that, then you weren't living your life right in the first place."

"That's true," I agree with my captor. I don't know why, but he sounds logical and I'm swimming in a sea of doubt.

He leaves, just like that, without another word.

I sit on the floor and I know it's for the last time.

I won't have to go through this cycle again. It will be over soon.

I open the last box.

There is a .45 revolver inside, and it gleams in the moonlight. I check the barrel. One bullet is in the chamber.

MY PEACE

The last journal page is folded beneath it.

I take a deep breath.

The drugs have dulled all of my senses. I'm not afraid. I'm not even sad. I'm an empty shell, and all I need is the last piece of this puzzle. I need to know.

I put the gun on my lap, and I pull out the paper. The ink on this page is fresh, a vibrant blue.

I've thought a lot over the years about why Susanna had acted like she did that night.

She rejected me, and refused to go with me, and I have to admit, that was a surprise. It took the wind out of my sails.

I know now, though, why she did it.

She must've thought I would kill her son.

She didn't trust me when I said I wouldn't.

If it had only been her and I, I know she would have gone with me in a split second. I would've saved her from that life. But her son came in, and she had to put on a show for him. She had to act like she didn't love me. I know it was a show. I saw how she'd looked at me every time I delivered their mail, day in and day out. She watched me, and she was lustful and she wanted me. I know it now, and I knew it then.

But some women, their instincts to be mothers overtakes everything else.

That's what happened that night.

I'm sure of it.

She fought for that snot-nosed kid. And in the end, I asked her why. Right before he rushed in and killed her, I asked her why she was fighting so hard for him.

She looked up at me, and her eyes were so wide and full of tears. And she said-

The paper is ripped here.
Her response is gone.
Leroy Ellison, being the monster that he is, is going to deny me my mother's last words. He brought me to the brink, then yanked it away. He was playing with me all along.

Rage billows in on clouds of red in my vision, and I find myself at the door, kicking and punching and yelling. No one hears, of course, and I turn, looking at the monitor. The men are in Zuzu's room, and they are taking her by the hand. The one who does the talking looks directly at the camera, directly at me.

He waves goodbye.

A cold pang runs through my heart, and if they went back on their word with the journal, then they will go back on their word with my daughter.

They aren't taking her back to her mother.

They are taking her out to kill her.

Fear for my daughter fights through the numbing fog of the drugs, and it emerges on top and I struggle with the door. I shout for Zuzu, to console her, to tell her that I love her, but it is all for nothing.

They are gone, and I am alone, and no one can hear me.

After a minute, I slump down on the bed, and I look outside, watching for them.

They walk outside and Zuzu is between them. She is barefoot and in her pajamas, and her blond hair gleams under the light of the moon. They are taking her out back.

MY PEACE

I pound on the glass and shout as loud as I can, but they don't turn around.

Are they going to kill my daughter by the lake? Will they distract her so she isn't afraid?

I am frozen in place as I watch. My hands are ice cold. The steel of the gun is even colder. I curl my fingers around the barrel.

I can't watch them kill Zuzu.

I can't do it.

I'm strong enough for anything but that.

I lift my face to the sky and I do something I haven't done in a long time.

I pray.

"God, please. Save my daughter. She doesn't deserve to pay for my sins. She's innocent and good. Everything that I'm not. Please… save her. And if you can't, for some reason, please make it painless. Make it quick. And then let she and I be together. Somewhere. Anywhere. Please take care of Mila. Please let her know that I loved her. More than life, more than anything. Please, God. I know I don't deserve an answered prayer, but if you could just do this. Please."

I am muttering but I have to believe that God knows my heart. He knows what I am trying to say.

"Please, forgive me for what I am about to do. I can't live without them. I can't live knowing that my daughter has died because of me. I'm not strong enough for that. Please forgive me."

I know they'll come back inside and kill me anyway.

When I go, it will be on my own terms.

I lower my chin, and I stare out the window. I remember walking on that beach with my wife, hand in hand. She smiled up at me, and she made everything good. The world is better with Mila in it. God knows that.

"I love you," I whisper to her. "I love you."

I picture her face, and I picture her smile, and I picture her answering me.

"I love you, too, Pax."

I lift the gun. The tip of it rests beneath my chin.

I take a breath.

My finger is on the trigger.

All I have to do is squeeze.

I take one more breath.

My last one.

Then…

Then…

The door opens.

I clench my teeth, getting ready to squeeze the trigger. They won't choose this for me. I'll do it myself. *I'll* pick the moment.

Maybe I'll make them watch. This can haunt their dreams.

They burst inside.

Only it's not *them*.

It's a SWAT team, in helmets and masks and vests.

"Put the gun down!" someone yells, and I'm frozen. Is this really happening? Am I imagining it? "Put the gun down!" they repeat, and so I do.

I lay it down on the floor.

The floor is cold under my fingers.

This is real.

I'm saved.

Or am I?

MY PEACE

As they bustle in and figure out who I am, and bundle me into a blanket, I feel more lost and alone than ever. I'm high as a kite, and I have no feelings. Not anymore.

I lost myself in this room.

I'll never be the same.

"My daughter," I mumble. "Is she alive?"

"Yes, Mr. Tate," they tell me. "She's fine. The EMTs are looking at her right now. What drugs have they given you?"

They can tell I'm high. I can't even tell them everything I've taken, everything that's in my system. There's too much to remember.

"What about my wife?" I ask him, and I'm afraid to hear the answer.

"She's alive," they say and I die a million deaths in relief. "She's on her way here to you."

But I can't.

I can't let her see me like this.

Chapter Thirty

Mila

"This is ridiculous," I tell the doctor again on the third day. "I surely don't need his permission."

I've been pacing the waiting room, day and night, and my husband refuses to allow me into his room. Gabe and Maddy have been with me for support, but I am crushed by the fact that Pax doesn't want to see me.

"He has given strict instructions that no one is allowed into his room," the doctor replies and he doesn't like it either. I can tell. "It's common with people who have been in captivity, even if it has only been ten days. He doesn't want you to see him in this state. He's not himself."

"Has he come through the physical withdrawals?" I ask hesitantly. I hate the thought of Pax being in pain. The doctor nods.

"He's through the worst of it. It will probably continue for up to a week, but the worst of it is past. The recovery process is mostly mental from here. He'll have to learn to resist the urges to use. It's a process."

I am stunned. My husband. My beautiful, strong husband, is lying in a hospital bed, addicted to drugs.

That's what *that monster* did to him.

My blood boils and I hope they manage to tie this to Leroy. So far, the detectives say that it looks like Natasha

MY PEACE

orchestrated it on her own. I know that's impossible. Leroy Ellison is behind this. He was just smart enough to hide it.

"Will you please tell him that I'm waiting here until he sees me? Tell him that I'm sleeping in the waiting room, and I'm not going anywhere."

The doctor hesitates, then nods. "I'll tell him. In the meantime, we do have counselors here. People you can talk to about your own ordeal."

"I'm fine," I assure him. "Maybe later. Right now, all I can concentrate on is my husband."

Zuzu is safe. I had smelled her hair and hugged her for an hour straight. I didn't want to let go of her, and I don't want her out of my sight even now. But I also don't want her here in this hospital. So she's at the hotel pool with Maddy and Gabe. I'll return to see her tonight, to eat dinner with her and hold her and smell her, before I come back to spend the night here.

Pax has to understand how important this is.

I have to show him.

I take my seat again.

I wait.

And wait.

And wait.

In the evening, Maddy and Gabe bring Zuzu to me, because I'd lost track of time. I'm still in a daze, and they know it.

Zuzu bounds into my arms, and she brings the sunshine with her.

"Mommy!" she cries, and she hugs me. "I missed you. Is daddy awake?"

We keep telling her that he is sleeping, and that's why she can't see him. We don't know what else to do.

"You just missed him, sweetheart," I tell her. "He misses you, too."

She nods her head, very confident of her father's love for her. "I drew him a picture."

I take it from her, and it is a family portrait. Me, Pax and Zuzu in the middle. She is holding a flower.

"He'll love it," she'll tells me seriously. I nod, and my eyes are filled with tears.

"He definitely will," I answer. "Can you go back to the hotel with aunt Maddy and uncle Gabe? Mommy wants to wait here for daddy to wake up again."

"Yes, Mommy," she says seriously. "Aunt Maddy is going to paint my nails."

I smile and Maddy hugs me. "It's all going to be fine," she tells me. "It is."

She takes Zuzu by the hand after I've kissed her three times. Gabe pauses next to me.

"I've seen this plenty of times," he tells me quietly. "In combat. He'll come around, Mila. He's in shock. He's been through a lot."

I nod. "I know."

"And so have you. Be easy on yourself. I need for you to get some sleep. Come to the hotel tonight. Rest."

I nod again. "Ok."

He's satisfied with that.

"Gabe?"

"Yeah, sweetie?"

"Thank you. For everything."

For saving my life. And Pax's. And Zuzu's.

He nods. "Always."

They leave, and I'm alone again.

MY PEACE

I wait for awhile longer, but the longer I stare at Zuzu's picture, the more my frustration grows. Our family consists of three people, soon to be four. Pax can't keep us away from him.

He can't.

I take the picture, and I slip down the hall. I wait until the nurses at the station are distracted, and then I slip through the double-doors. He's in room three-fifteen, so I count the rooms down as I pass, and before I know it, I'm in front of his.

I lift the latch.

I push the door open.

Pax is in the bed, his eyes closed.

My breath leaves my body in a whoosh.

Déjà vu floods through me.

Once upon a time, I'd walked into a hospital room and found Pax like this, hooked up to IVs and in a hospital bed.

Today, though, my beautiful husband's face is battered and bruised. There is a bandage across his nose and I assume it's broken. I watched the beating they gave him. I knew it had to leave a mark.

But until this moment, I had no idea how much so.

His face is blue and purple, his cheek swollen.

His eyes are closed… until… they aren't.

He looks at me, quiet and still, his gaze golden.

"Red," he murmurs, and for a moment, just a moment, he is happy to see me. His eyes light up, and he reaches for me. But then, just as quickly, he masks it.

He drops his hand, and the light in his eyes fades.

"You're not supposed to be here."

I rush to him, grabbing his arm, trying to hug him.

"Babe, I thought they were going to kill you. And you're alive, and I just want to hold you. Please."

He softens for a moment, and holds me to him, and I hear his heart beat even though I'm slumped over the bed rail.

"I love you," I tell him. "I love you. I watched you on the TV monitor, and all I wanted to do was touch you. And now I am." I stroke his strong arm, and I see that it is littered with needle tracks. Bruises and dried blood. I swallow hard. This is real. It happened.

He's quiet and I lift my head.

"Why don't you want to see me?"

Pain ricochets through my heart at the expression on his face. It's so… detached. Forcibly detached. He's doing this on purpose. But why?

"You can't be around me," he says simply. "You or Zuzu. I'm… not good for anyone."

I'm startled. "Pax, you are the best man I know. You're not thinking clearly right now."

He shakes his head and stares out the window, away from me.

"You didn't see what I did. I caved in right away, Mi. They wanted me to do drugs, and I did them. I slipped into addiction so easily. Too easily. I wasn't strong enough. I'll hurt you again and again. I can't be with you."

He swallows and his eyes are red.

"Babe, you don't know what you're saying. Natasha told me… she laced the muscle relaxers she gave you. She purposely was leading you down the path to addiction. They orchestrated everything."

"But I'm the one who chose to use," he says simply. "I didn't have to."

MY PEACE

"I spoke with the detectives," I tell him hesitantly. "They told me what happened. Those men *made* you, Pax. They threatened Zuzu. I don't see that you had much of a choice."

"They were going to kill her anyway," he says quietly. "I knew that from the beginning. I guess I just hoped..." his voice trails off.

"She's alive because of what you did," I tell him. "You delayed it long enough for the police to come. You saved her life, Pax."

He shakes his head, refusing to believe it. I know him. I know he's in a dark place right now, a place where he is unable to hear good things. I haven't seen him in this place in years, and it terrifies me now.

"They're doing surgery on your knee soon," I tell him. "Are you in pain?"

"Yeah."

"I'm so sorry, babe."

He looks away.

"You've got to leave, Mila. I can't have you here."

"But why? I love you. I need you. And you need me, too."

"I can't need you," he says, and his voice is so husky and broken. "It's not fair to you anymore. Walk out the door, Mila. Don't look back. I told you once that I wasn't good for you, and neither of us paid attention. And look what has happened. A wolf can only pretend to be harmless for so long before the truth comes out."

His words hurt me so much, they cut deep. "You said love never fails," I tell him, and God, *this can't be happening.* "Did you lie?"

I'm stunned and I don't know what to do. Pax swallows hard.

"No. Love hasn't failed, babe. *I* did."

The words cut through the air, the sharpest of knives and they twist into my heart, until I can't breathe. My lungs are a vacuum and they are empty.

"You didn't," I argue, but he won't listen.

He gestures around us at the sterile room. "I'm here," he says simply. "And next, I'm going to rehab. You deserve better, Mila. And you're going to get it."

"I deserve *you*," I insist, but his eyes are closed now, and he presses the nurse's call button. She appears immediately, elderly and stern.

"Mrs. Tate doesn't want to leave and I'm tired," Pax says quietly. "Can you show her out?"

The woman stares down at me sympathetically, but she has no choice other than to do as he asks.

"Wait," I tell her. I hand Pax Zuzu's picture. "Your daughter made this for you."

His eyes well up and he looks away.

"I'm not leaving you, Pax," I tell him over my shoulder. "I'm not going anywhere."

He doesn't answer. When I look over my shoulder, as the door closes, he is still, his lashes on his cheek, and Zuzu's picture clutched to his chest.

MY PEACE

Chapter Thirty-One

Pax

Watching Mila walk away is the hardest thing I've ever had to do.

Pushing the button for the nurse was hard.

But shaking her off my arm, and sending her out… that was excruciating. The rejection on her face…

It's for the best, I tell myself. *It's for the best.*

I live in a place now that is unsuitable for them. I live in the dark, in the oblivion, and I'll never be safe from it. I'll never be able to say that I'm impermeable to slipping.

I never thought I would. But I did.

I'll never make that arrogant mistake again.

I'll never think I'm stronger than I am. I'll never doubt my ability to fall. I've fallen hard. And I'm not sure if I'm getting back up. I don't deserve it.

The paper in my hand is fragile, and it's priceless. I gaze at it, and I feel the tears start to swell. Me, Mila and Zuzu stare back from the page in crayon form. Zu had made Mila's belly round, to show the baby that will be growing there, and I can't swallow. I can barely breathe.

I prop it up on the stand next to the table, and I fall asleep again, because sleep is medicine.

It heals my broken body, and when I sleep, the pain of sending Mila away is dulled. It's always there, buried in my heart, but when I'm not conscious, it's not as sharp. It's not as real.

I'm resentful when I wake to find my father standing above me.

He's troubled, concerned, and he's holding my hand. He hasn't done that since I was a child.

"I was afraid," he says simply.

I nod. "I was too."

"You're ok." He says it as a statement. I shrug. I don't know about that.

"You're ok," he says again, more firmly this time. As if saying so will make it true.

"I don't know," I tell him. "I'm an addict. Remember telling me that years ago? I denied it then. I said I was just a user. But I'm not. I'm an addict. I lied to myself then, and I lied to you. I buried it instead of dealing with it, and now here we are."

"This isn't your fault," he says and his voice is soft. I pull my hand away.

"On the surface, no. It isn't. But deep down, it is. If I had dealt with my shit years ago, I mean, truly dealt with it, I wouldn't be here now. I wouldn't be hooked to a methadone drip. I wouldn't have just crushed my wife. But I didn't. And so here I am, and I did."

My father's face is pained, and he tries to reason with me, but he loves me. He's trying to shield me.

"I need you to take care of Alexander Holdings," I tell him. "Can you do that? Can you work with Peter and figure something out? I'm obviously not in the right frame of mind for it right now."

"Of course," he says quickly. "That's not a problem. I'm more worried about you than the business…"

MY PEACE

"Don't be," I tell him abruptly. "I'm going to handle it."

"You and Mila have both been through so much," he finally answers. "Mila has too. She thought they had killed you. She's hurting too, son."

God, that hurts. It stabs me deep in the heart and the knife twists round and round.

"It's better that I hurt her this one last time than to keep hurting her forever," I manage to say.

"You're wrong," he says.

"You don't get it," I tell him sharply. "If I'd admitted to myself years ago that I was an addict, I could've learned to deal with it. With the issues that made me use. Instead, I just stopped using, and I pretended that it wasn't an issue. It was. And it is. And here I am."

"Pax. You stopped using. That was what you were supposed to do," my father says. "You did the right thing. Sometimes, people have latent issues that rear their heads later. You didn't know. You had no way of knowing that you had other things to deal with. But what... what exactly do you feel you didn't deal with?"

I can't answer.

I can't tell him that after all of those hours of therapy, I still feel at fault for my mother's death. That I can't understand the fact that I was a kid and I was just trying to protect my mother. My head knows it, but my heart... my heart isn't listening. And my heart is what drives the addiction.

So I don't answer him. I close my eyes instead.

After a long time, my father's voice is quiet.

"There are a lot of people who love you, son. All of us stand behind you. You're not alone."

He leaves. I hear the door close, and I open my eyes.

I *am* alone.

I'm in a hospital room alone, and I chose this.

It's a hell of my own making.

***

I spend a week in the hospital recuperating. They do the surgery on my knee, and I'm up and doing PT the very next day. I refuse any kind of pain medication, and the pain is excruciating.

I push through it.

It reminds me that I'm alive. It's punishing. I deserve it.

After I'm released, I go straight to a rehab facility. My father arranged it, and Roger drives me.

"Thank you for saving my wife," I tell him, because this is the first time I've seen him since everything happened. "We owe our lives to you. It's a debt that I can never repay."

Roger dismisses it. "Anyone would've done the same," he tells me. "You're a good man, sir. Just like your grandfather. It's my honor to help."

"Please drive my wife wherever she needs to go, ok?" I ask him as he pulls up to the facility. "Look out for her. Will you do that?"

"Of course, sir. Again, it's my honor. I'll watch out for her like you would yourself… right up until you come home."

I don't tell him that I'm not coming home.

"Thank you," I say quietly instead. "You're a good man."

MY PEACE

I limp into rehab, leaning on a cane.

I breathe in the pain, and breathe out the anger. I am a dragon, and my air is fire.

They show me to my room, and it's nicer than I had wanted, a corner room with a view of gardens. I hadn't wanted anything fancy. I wanted a cot and a toilet. Leave it my father to ensure my comfort.

I toss my bag into the closet and I flop onto the bed, face-down into the pillows.

I stay this way for a long time. I don't even know how long.

"Are you ok?"

There is a muffled voice, and I wave my hand for them to go away. They don't.

"Are you ok?" They are more insistent now.

I sit up.

It's a woman.

"I thought this was a men's only facility," I tell her, rubbing my face. She's middle-aged, soft-spoken. She's dressed well, classy. Hounds-tooth slacks and a cream-colored turtleneck. Her hair is pulled into a ponytail at the nape of her neck.

"It is," she answered. "So don't tell on me."

She comes in, and pours a glass of water from a pitcher, then hands it to me. "You need to drink this. It flushes out toxins."

I snort. "It's going to take more than that," I say, but I take the glass and gulp the liquid down. I set the glass down, and then it occurs to me. "You're my therapist?" I guess.

She sits in the chair next to the bed.

"What if I am? Will you talk to me?"

"Not today," I answer. "I'm very tired."

"You've been through a lot," she agrees. "Why don't you rest tonight, get something to eat, and I'll be back in the morning."

It's a firm suggestion, said gently.

"Ok. We'll see how I feel in the morning."

She nods and slips out the door.

I pull Zuzu's drawing out of my bag, and prop it on my nightstand.

Then I fall back asleep.

MY PEACE

Chapter Thirty-Two

My therapist is back in the morning, this time with two cups of coffee. She hands me one.

I sip at it, and I rub my face. She hadn't even given me time to wake-up.

"This is an early session," I point out. She smiles.

"I work best in the morning."

"I don't," I reply honestly. She smiles.

"Tell me about you," she suggests.

I pause. I don't want to. But I know that until I get this over-with, it's going to be like this every day.

"Where do you want me to start?"

"The beginning is always good."

So that's where I begin.

I tell her about everything. From my mother's murder, to my childhood with my father, to my relationship with Mila, to my marriage, and through my captivity.

"That leaves us with today," she points out. We've been talking for two hours already.

"Yeah."

"Why are you here?"

"Because I don't know what else to do. I have this… monster inside of me. And it will rear its head from now until eternity if I don't figure something out."

"If we can figure it out, will you go back to Mila?" she asks gently.

I stare straight ahead. "I'll never risk her safety again."

"You know, Pax. Bad things happen in the world. They aren't all tied to you. Meaning… you don't cause them. You don't control them. You understand that, don't you?"

"You're kidding, right? The bad things that have happened to us have been *directly* tied to me, and decisions that I have made."

"That's how life is, though," she says. Her voice is gentle and soothing, and I wonder how much training that entailed… to master just the right tone. "Sometimes, things happen that are out of our control. We must deal with those things, but we shouldn't push our loved ones away."

"You don't understand," I tell her.

"So help me," she counters.

"Later. I can't right now. I've had enough today."

She stands up.

"You have a group therapy meeting in thirty minutes."

I nod, and she's gone. She takes the empty coffee cups with her, and leaves me with troubled thoughts.

I miss my wife.

I miss my daughter.

I miss my life.

I sigh, and lay my head down on the pillow.

I don't mean to fall asleep, but I do, because my body is ragged and exhausted and needs to heal. While I sleep, I dream.

I dream of my wife. My dreams are rich and colorful and filled with her.

When I wake, I feel emptier than I ever have before.

***

MY PEACE

Group therapy feels pretty useless today, because I don't feel like I belong.

I sit back and observe, and listen to the other addicts share their issues, their triggers. None of it seems to apply to me. For years, I didn't have the urge to use.

Talking about it though, with them, it makes me ache for the sting of the needle. It's ironic. The very thing that is supposed to heal me, is making me want the poison all the more.

When it's my turn, they wait for me to speak. I look around the circle, and they're all waiting, and I have nothing to say.

"I'm Pax, and I'm an addict," I say slowly. "I was held against my will, and forced to take drugs. The guy who arranged the whole thing wanted to take everything important in my life. My sobriety was just one of those things."

I can tell that some don't believe me. I get it. A lot of addicts make excuses and even make up stories to excuse their drug use. They don't want to admit that they themselves are at fault, because then they themselves will have to fix it.

I understand.

That used to be me.

"Why do you want to get clean?" someone asks, and I know it's an important question. You have to have a reason, in order to do it. That's true of every goal in life. I shake my head.

"I'm tired of being chased by demons. I'm tired of being a danger to everyone around me. I'm a ticking time bomb."

They accept that, and move on to the next person. I sit like a piece of wood for the rest of the meeting. I feel out of place here, and I don't know why. I guess it's because I don't want to identify as an addict.

But it's what I am.

***

"That's normal," my therapist tells me the next morning. "Your addiction is a part of you that you don't completely understand. Let's work through it together, shall we?"

I nod, and she continues.

"Your childhood. You've told me that you felt like your father didn't like you."

"I used to. When I was growing up. Now I know that he was just really struggling with my mother's death."

"That's the fact of it," she agrees. "But when you were a boy, you didn't know that. You felt rejected, did you not? You felt like you couldn't trust your own father to want you. Correct?"

I think on that, and then I nod. "Yeah. I guess I did."

"And your mother left you. She couldn't help it, but she did. And you felt extreme guilt because you knew that it was *your hand* that killed her. You felt so much guilt about that that you suppressed all memories of it."

I nod. "Yes."

"So, you were a very troubled little boy, and no one knew it."

MY PEACE

"I've got baggage," I agree. "We know that. That's why I'm here."

"You expressed that baggage in your early twenties by using drugs and being sexually promiscuous. You went through women like water, using them and tossing them aside."

That makes me cringe. It feels like someone else, not me, who did that. But it's true. I did it. I nod.

"Where are you going with this?"

"You felt like you didn't deserve something real," she finally points out. "It was never about those women. It was about you, and how you felt about yourself."

I think about that. "I always gravitated to the drug users," I tell her. "I guess because they didn't expect much from me. They wanted to use. I was able to give them that."

"And in return, they slept with you," she says, and it sounds so ugly out loud. "They gave you the façade of intimacy, the barest amount. Just enough to keep you functioning, pretending that your life was just how you wanted it."

"It was how I wanted it at the time," I argue.

"You only thought that, I think," she says thoughtfully, chewing at her lip. "You couldn't bear rejection of someone real. Like you felt your father had rejected you."

I'm stunned by that.

All along, I felt that my issues were caused by my mother dying, which didn't make a lot of sense because she couldn't help that. She didn't choose death.

But my father... he chose to draw away from me. He paid for my school, he paid for everything I needed, he bailed me out of trouble time and again. But he was never able to give me what I needed the most.

He was never able to be vulnerable and show that he loved me.

"He does now," I tell her, almost defensively. "He's a good father."

"Yes," she agrees. "I can tell. But when he was younger, and he was in mourning, he couldn't manage himself, let alone his relationship with you. And you were so small. It was a formative time for you. And now you have a deep-seeded fear of rejection."

That's why I always chose bar whores for years. They wouldn't reject me.

The revelation is huge.

"That's enough for today," she decides, standing up and stretching. "We'll meet again in the morning."

I nod. "Okay. Thank you."

When she's gone, I curl up in my bed, and I stare at the wall.

I miss my wife. I miss my daughter.

I reach for the phone in a moment of weakness. The receiver is in my hand before I gain control of myself and put it back down.

No.

I'm strong enough to do this alone.

I won't drag them into my shit.

I fall sleep, and the oblivion of sleep swirls around me like a drug.

MY PEACE

Chapter Thirty-Three

When I wake, a stamped letter is sitting on my nightstand.

The mail cart must've gone by.

I recognize Mila's handwriting on the envelope, feminine and swirly.

I swallow hard, and open it.

There is no note. Only a ring drops out. Her mother's ring.

LOVE NEVER FAILS. Those words are inscribed on the inside, and my heart pounds. God, I miss my wife.

"What's that?" the therapist breezes through the door, her eye on my hand. I hold up the ring.

"Mila's parents had a rough marriage, tumultuous. But her mother believed that Love never fails, and had her ring inscribed. Mila wears it. She sent it to me. As a message."

"That her love for you hasn't failed," the therapist says slowly.

I nod. "Yeah." My throat feels tight.

"Your wife is pregnant, isn't she?" she asks gently. I nod again.

"Yeah."

"You don't seem like the kind of man to walk out on his family," she says. Just hearing it put like that sends a shiver up my spine and angers me.

"I'm not running out on my family" I say through my teeth. "I'm protecting them. I'm not balanced right now. I might not ever be. At any moment, I could slip and use again. If I'm not strong enough to stay sober."

"How long were you sober this last time?" she asks curiously.

"Over five years."

"And why did you start using again?" She knows why. But I humor her.

"I took pills for my knee. It needed surgery. And then, well, Leroy Ellison arranged to make me use drugs. He wanted revenge."

It sounds so ridiculous out loud. Like something from a movie.

She stares at me. "You just said, *he made you.*"

"He did."

"So you wouldn't have chosen it," she points out.

"But I chose to take the muscle relaxers for my knee," I tell her and I'm angry now. I want her to stop trying to make me seem better than I am.

"But those were laced with methamphetamines," she reminds me.

"Yes, but…"

"No buts," she says gently, yet firmly. "They were laced with the most addictive substance known to man."

"Yes," I admit. "But…"

"No buts," she says, getting up. "We'll resume this session after dinner."

She leaves, and I'm not hungry. I slip Mila's ring on my pinkie.

MY PEACE

It makes me feel close to her. Like I'm close, but still far enough away not to hurt her. It rips my heart out. I close my eyes and rest until the therapist comes back.

***

The therapist is relentless.

"Do you see the parallels?" she asks me after an hour. "Between the way you are behaving right now, and how your father behaved when you were small?"

I'm silent.

She smiles. "You see it. He checked out. He felt that distance between the two of you would protect you from his grief. He felt that he would hurt you with words that he couldn't seem to control. That he might accidentally blame you for killing your mother. He knew it wasn't your fault, but his heart was still healing. So he put distance between you.

And here you are. You know in your head that your addiction right now isn't something you chose. But your heart is telling you to protect your family from harm."

"The harm is me," I tell her. "I'm the danger."

"Life is dangerous," she points out. "There is a risk in everything. But you are a good man. You are strong and loyal and true. That's all we can ask of you, Pax. That's all anyone can ask."

"You don't understand," I tell her helplessly.

"But I do," she argues. "More than you know."

For some reason that lump is back in my throat, the one that I can't swallow.

"You feel that you aren't valuable enough to take a risk for," she says ever so gently. "That Mila is better off without you, even though she loves you more than her own life. She has told you that numerous times, you said. And your daughter, and your unborn child, they need their father. Just like you needed yours."

"But I could hurt them," I tell her hotly.

She nods. "Yes, you could. And you will hurt them if you don't go back home. That will do more damage than anything else you could do."

We sit in silence for a few minutes as I soak that in, as I consider it.

Could she possibly be right?

Could my absence truly be worse than anything else?

It's hard for me to comprehend.

"I took the liberty of getting something for you," she finally says, and she pulls out an envelope. "I called the detective in charge of the investigation, and he sent this to me. It arrived yesterday."

She hands the last journal page, the one I'd told her about. The one with the bottom torn off.

It's hard to look at it, because when I do, I remember sitting on the floor with a gun pressed to my chin, ready to take my own life.

"Read it aloud to me," she says. "I know it's hard, because saying the words gives them power. But please. Read them aloud."

I stare at the words, and reluctantly give them my voice.

I've thought a lot over the years about why Susanna had acted like she did that night.

MY PEACE

She rejected me, and refused to go with me, and I have to admit, that was a surprise. It took the wind out of my sails.

I know now, though, why she did it.
She must've felt that I would kill her son.
She didn't trust me when I said I wouldn't.

If it had only been her and I, I know she would have gone with me in a split second. I would've saved her from that life. But her son came in, and she had to put on a show for him. She had to act like she didn't love me like I loved her. I know it was a show. I saw how she'd looked at me every time I delivered their mail, day in and day out. She watched me, and she was lustful and she wanted me. I know it now, and I knew it then.

But some women, their instincts to be mothers overtakes everything else.

That's what happened that night.
I'm sure of it.

She fought for that snot-nosed kid. And in the end, I asked her why. Right before he rushed in and killed her, I asked her why she was fighting so hard for him.

She looked up at me, and her eyes were so wide and full of tears. And she said-

I stop, because that's the end.

The therapist looks at m, and I swear her eyes are moist with unshed tears.

"What do you think she said?"

I shake my head, and put the page down. "I don't know."

"Don't you?" she asks.

"No, I don't. Maybe she said that she loved me."

That thought constricts every one of my muscles, and I feel like a snake is trying to squeeze the life out of my body, a giant vise grip and my ribs… they can't breathe.

I suck in a breath.

The therapist lays a piece of paper in my lap.

I look down.

It's a small torn piece. It matches the journal page.

The missing piece.

My heart pounds. "Turn it over and read it," she says softly.

With shaking fingers, I do.

"He's worth it."

MY PEACE

Chapter Thirty-Four

"And she said… he's worth it," I repeat, and my heart. God, it feels like it's going to explode with an emotion I don't recognize.

"You're worth it," the therapist tells me simply. "Your mother knew it. She knew that you were so valuable, and so loved by her, that she would willingly give her life for you. She wanted you to live. She wanted you to thrive and be healthy. Because *you're worth it.*"

"I'm worth it," I say aloud, and the words feel foreign. I'm almost thirty years old, and I never once have felt like I'm worth it. I realize that now, in this very heavy moment.

"You're worth it."

I stare at the therapist, and she stares back.

"Do you believe it?"

"I don't know."

"That is your task," she says finally. "To get to a place where you believe you're worth it. Until you do, you won't have peace."

"My name means peace," I tell her, off-hand. "My mother always said I was her peace."

She nods. "I know."

I don't remember telling her that, but I don't say it.

"I know your wife feels like you're worth it," she says. "And your daughter. And your unborn baby will someday feel it, too. You are a good man, Pax Tate. I knew you would be, and you are."

I stare at the floor, and tears threaten to fall. I don't know why. Hearing someone say that I have value... it has power.

"Give your wife the chance to love you," she suggests. "She loves you more than anything, and you love her, too. That is what life is all about."

She stands up.

"Our sessions are over," she says. "You'll continue with the group sessions for the rest of your stay here. It's been very nice to speak with you. Can I hug you?"

I nod, and she bends, pulling me into a warm hug.

She feels soft and familiar, and when she turns to leave, I realize something.

She smells like honeysuckle.

"You never told me your name," I point out as she leaves.

She pauses, staring over her shoulder.

"No, I guess I didn't."

She's gone but the scent of honeysuckle remains, and I'm stunned, and it's a coincidence.

"It's a coincidence," I say aloud. "I'm losing it."

I'm just taking old feelings and pinning them on her, like wishful thinking.

I spend the afternoon thinking about the things she said, and pondering. Maybe she's right. Maybe I do have value.

Maybe I *am* worth it.

After group, I pull aside the main counselor. "I'd like to have one more individual session with my therapist, if that's possible," I tell her.

MY PEACE

She stares at me, confused.

"You haven't begun your individual therapy yet. That begins in week two."

"But… I've been speaking to a woman," I tell her. "Slim, blond, middle-aged, classy-looking."

She shakes her head. "We don't have anyone here who fits that description."

"Are you sure?" I ask weakly.

"Quite," she nods.

Somehow, I make it back to my room on my weak legs, and it still smells vaguely of honeysuckle inside. Light and soft, not the cloying scent that Natasha had worn. I look around, at the four walls and empty room.

"This can't be," I say aloud, because saying words aloud gives them power.

But I know for a fact that I've been speaking with someone. I'm not imagining it.

I'm shaky as I sit on the bed.

I'm shaky as I remember the past few days, and how familiar and warm I had felt while speaking with her. She made me feel comfortable. Safe. Secure. Like my subconscious was picking up things that *I* wasn't.

I am overwhelmed. And while I've never believed in anything unexplainable, I want to believe in this. I want to believe that my mother was here.

It gives me hope, and hope is priceless.

I pick up the torn paper lying on my nightstand.

He's worth it.

Maybe I am.

I pick up the phone.

I call my wife.

Courtney Cole

MY PEACE

Chapter Thirty-Five

Mila

"Babe?"

The voice coming from the phone is surreal. Husky.

"Pax?" I sit in the nearest chair, and my fingers immediately begin to shake. "Are you ok?"

"Yeah. I… I don't know what to say. I miss you."

"I miss you, too," I tell him quickly. "Are you ok?"

"I'm an addict, Red," he says solemnly, but he called me Red.

He called me Red. My heart sings with the sound of it.

"I know," I tell him. "But we can deal with it. We can, Pax."

"I know. I'm sorry. I didn't mean to make you feel like I abandoned you. I'm so sorry. For everything."

My throat chokes up. "Does this mean you're coming home?"

There's a pause. "Yes. If you'll have me. As soon as I'm done with the program."

I cry now. I can't help it. I sob and my shoulders shake, and Pax tries to comfort me from the other end of the line.

"Babe, it's ok. Don't cry. I don't want you to cry."

"What changed?" I'm finally able to ask.

"It's hard to explain," he answers. "My mom... she just told me that I'm worth it. The journal... Leroy kept a journal. And in the end, he asked her why she was sacrificing herself for me, and she said that I was worth it."

"You are," I tell him quickly, and God, this makes my heart break. "You are."

"So," he continues. "I'm going to try to come to terms with that. To really understand, I mean, deep down, that I have worth and value. I don't think I've ever believed that was true."

"Even after we've been together?" I ask, confused. How is that possible?

He's slow to answer. "Not deep down," he says. "I think I've always felt like I didn't deserve you. Or anything good, actually. That I'd just lucked out that you loved me."

"That's not true," I argue. "I'm the lucky one, Pax."

"I love you so much," he tells me, and his voice is broken. I try to imagine what he's doing. He's sitting, I think. Hunched over the phone. "I can't believe I've done this. I can't believe I'm here."

"Babe, this wasn't your fault. Please believe that."

"I'm trying," he answers. "Will you come on visiting day? To see me?"

"Try to keep me away," I tell him through my tears. "I was already planning on being there."

We talk for a little while longer, and my heart threatens to explode with my love for this man. Everything else that has happened fades away, and all that matters is Pax.

"The baby?" he asks. "It's ok?"

"Yes. We're both fine. Zuzu is fine. She misses you, but I told her that you're getting better."

"I am," he tells me. "I am. Tell her I'll be home soon."

MY PEACE

"I will." My throat chokes up again. "I love you so much."

"I love you, too."

We hang up, and I suddenly feel stronger than I ever have before. We're going to survive this. Pax will survive it.

***

I'm waiting in the commons room of the rehab facility ten minutes before visiting hours begin. I'm fidgety and my foot taps on the floor.

"Is this seat taken?"

A voice from behind me. My husband's voice.

I turn, and leap from the chair, and throw my arms around his neck.

He smells like wood, and the outdoors and man.

He laughs into my hair, and his hands are stroking my back, and his arms are strong.

"I missed you," he tells me, his lips against my cheek. "Thank you for coming."

"Trust me, you couldn't have kept me away."

"I know. I tried that before. It didn't work," he agrees.

I snarl at him. "Don't do that again. Whatever happens, we face it together. Do you understand?"

He nods. "Yeah. I do."

I hold his hand as he gives me a tour, showing me the grounds and his room.

"Is everything all right at home?" he asks as we sit on his bed. I nod.

"Yeah. Roger is fussing about like a woman."

Pax laughs. "I told him to keep an eye on you."

"Sasha is trying to hire a new housekeeper for me, but I'm not ready yet," I tell him. "I just… I can't."

She can't open our home to a stranger again. I completely understand.

"At some point, we'll need one, if we stay in that house," I point out. "It's too big to manage alone."

"Do you want to stay there?" I ask him. He shrugs.

"I don't know. Do you? You were the one locked in our room."

"For some reason, I haven't struggled with that," I tell him. "The only thing that bothers me is the living room. Sasha had the rugs replaced, because of the blood, but I've kept the doors closed and we don't go in there. It feels….well, it's got bad energy."

"I'm going to talk to my father," he decides. "We'll see what can be done."

"I don't care about that right now,'" I tell him. "I just want to spend time with you."

He pulls me into him, against his chest, and he holds me there. I listen to his heart for minutes and minutes, before I speak again.

"I want to come to therapy with you," I tell him. "I want us to face this together, as much as possible."

He's quiet, then he nods. "If you'd like."

"I would."

So that's what we do.

I come for therapy with him three times a week for the remainder of his three-week stay in rehab.

He has to do PT on his knee during the day, and individual sessions as well, so he stays busy.

Every day he gets stronger. I see it. It's a visible improvement.

MY PEACE

His father visits him, and when he drops by the house afterward, he's pleased.

"He's better than I've ever seen him," he announces as he sits at the kitchen table with me for a cup of tea. "He looks so healthy."

"He *is* healthy," I say proudly. "He's doing so well."

"Did he tell you that I attended therapy with him?" Paul asks me. This is news. I shake my head.

"No."

"I did. Twice. He had some pent-up issues with me, issues he didn't even know he had. After Susanna died... I wasn't very available to him. I'm sorry for that. I wasn't handling my grief, and it affected him. It has affected you, as well. I'm terribly sorry for that."

I reach out and squeeze his arm. "You didn't mean to hurt him," I say, and I completely believe that. "Grief does strange things to a person."

"It does,' he agrees. "It really does. I was hurting the most important person in my life, and didn't even realize it."

"Well, from now on, we only go forward," I decide, sipping my tea. "And we don't dwell on the past. Is that a deal?"

"Absolutely," Paul agrees. He pauses. "Also, I looked at William's will again. There's a clause in it concerning force majeure."

"Force majeure?" I stare at him.

"Yeah. It's a set of unforeseen circumstances that might prevent someone from fulfilling a contract. It's usually something natural, like a hurricane or something. But sometimes, in a case like this, it can be applied."

"A case like this?"

"William stipulated that you had to live in his house. Given the circumstances that you were held captive in it, and someone died in it, I believe that force majeure would apply. I know that William wouldn't want to force you into staying there under these conditions. I'm going to speak with the judge overseeing the estate, and see if he agrees. If he does, you can sell, and buy a new house, while Pax can still take over his grandfather's business and fortune, as planned."

Relief floods me. "That would be a blessing," I tell him. "I hate it here."

"I know you do," he answers. "But hopefully soon, we'll get it straightened out."

We finish our tea in silence, and as Paul stands up to go, he turns to me.

"Thank you for loving my son so much," he tells me, and his voice is a little choked up. "You've given him the life that I always dreamed he would have."

"He's given me the life *I* always dreamed I would have," I tell him. "So I'm grateful to you for bringing him into this world."

He hugs me, and then he's gone.

I watch Zuzu through the window, running and playing with Chelcie, and I cup my belly with my hand. Soon, she'll have a brother or sister to play with. And we'll be in a brand-new home, with a brand-new beginning.

MY PEACE

Chapter Thirty-Six

Pax

Three weeks of therapy has passed slowly and quickly at the same time.

I would be lying if I said I didn't crave heroin. I do. It will be a struggle for some time to come. I know that. But I also know I'm strong enough to withstand it.

I'm worth it.

I believe that now.

I'm ready to go home to be with my wife and daughter, and at the same time, I'm afraid. I'm afraid of failing them.

I take a deep breath as I pack my bag.

I put the picture Zuzu made for me on top, where it won't get crumpled.

When Roger comes to pick me up, Mila isn't accompanying him. My father steps out of the car. I'm disappointed, but try not to show it. He laughs.

"Expecting someone else?"

I grimace. Was it that obvious?"

He smiles. "You've been away from your wife for weeks. Trust me, I understand. I'm taking you to her though. She wants you to come to her."

"Where is she?"

"It's a surprise."

"Mila does love surprises," I nod. I'm so happy to be leaving and going home, that I don't even mind not knowing what's going on. The car glides away from the curb and my father chats idly about business, and I only halfway listen.

I'm going home to my wife.

That's all that matters.

I'm strong enough for this, I remind myself for the twentieth time today. *I'm strong enough.*"

The car weaves among the traffic to the other side of the city, and then out of traffic into the outskirts of town. We pass through a gate, guarded by a security guard. It's a housing development, with homes spaced very far apart from each other.

It's nice. It's upscale.

My curiosity is piqued.

We pull into one long driveway, a drive paved with stone. The car weaves up the curve, and stops in front of a beautiful house.

Not small, not too large, it's perfect. It's exterior is stone, and it's solid and graceful. I lift an eyebrow at my father. He shakes his head.

"Go find out for yourself."

Roger opens my door and I'm out the door. My knee is still stiff, even with the PT, so I can only move so fast, but I get to the front door as fast as I can.

Mila opens it before I can ring the doorbell, her face radiant.

"Welcome home, babe," she says, gesturing me in with a grand sweep of her arm. "I hope you love it."

I'm speechless as I enter, treading over gleaming wood floors. It's comfortable here. Very nice, yet still very comfortable. We pass through a formal dining room and a butler's pantry and into a large kitchen.

MY PEACE

"Your father made it so we could sell your grandfather's house," Mila tells me. "I hope you don't mind that I've bought this one. I wanted you to come home to a new start. Someplace we can start fresh with new memories, not ugly old ones."

"I've never been happier," I tell her honestly. She grins.

"Let me show you our bedroom."

She leads me into the master suite, and it's awash with grays and creams, the light streams in, and it's all very soft, very sophisticated. "The shower is extra tall for you," she tells me, as she leads me in. And it is. It's the perfect size for me, and there's a soaking tub for Mila.

"We're going to be happy here," I tell her. She nods. "Yes, we will."

We make our way through the rest of the house, through Zuzu's room and what will be the nursery.

"I can't believe you got this taken care of in just a couple of weeks," I finally tell her as we sit in our new living room. It is decorated in a warm coastal style, laid back and casual.

My father pipes in. "Your wife is a force to be reckoned with."

I glance at her. "That, I know."

She laughs, and Zuzu sits on my lap, her blond hair against my chest. I pull at her curls gently, and I don't forget the one that I have in my pocket. I've been carrying it with me to remember the things that matter the most.

"This room is missing one thing," I tell my wife. Her head snaps up.

"I forgot something?"

I whisper into Zuzu's ear, and she grins, then runs off. She returns a few minutes later, the picture that she had drawn of our family in her hand.

"I'd like to get this framed and put in here," I say, and Mila's smile lights up the room.

"I think that's perfect."

We sit and chat until well past Zuzu's bedtime, and then my father excuses himself to leave.

"Don't be a stranger," I tell him as he hugs me.

"I won't," he promises.

Mila and I take Zuzu to bed, and tuck her in. We read her a story, and then two, and finally, we tiptoe out into our own bedroom down the hall.

After Mila takes a bath, and I take a shower, we climb into our new bed.

"I thought this moment would never come," I tell Mila, and she collapses into me, her heat and her softness meshed against my hardness.

"Me either," she admits. "I was ready for bedtime."

I start to kiss her, and she kisses me back with soft lips before she pulls away.

"I need you to promise that you're never going to try and face life without me again," she says. "We're a team. For better or for worse, always."

"Always," I agree. "I promise."

And then…

Then…

I attack her. I crush her lips to mine, and I inhale her the way I've been wanting to for weeks. She smells so familiar, so mine, and I soak her up, like sunshine on a cold day.

MY PEACE

She reacts, and her legs lift up and around my hips and my breathing is already ragged.

She slides her hand along my chest and kisses me hard. "I don't want to hurt you," I tell her because she's pregnant, and I'm frantic already.

"You won't," she promises. "Make love to me, Pax. I've been waiting for weeks."

So I do.

I gently make love to my wife. She is mine, and I am hers, and we come together in our bed like we will never see each other again. Something we've certainly learned is that tomorrow is never promised.

She arches her back and presses into me and I slide inside, gently, easily, then with more and more thrust.

"I love you so much," I breathe into her neck. "I love you so much."

"I love you, too."

She shudders against me and moans my name and I can't hold out any more.

My entire body shakes with my release.

We make love three more times in the night. Gently, rougher, then gently again. We are two people who can't get enough of each other. I get as close as I can, pulling her skin to mine, but it will never be enough.

By morning, we are a tousled mess.

Zuzu runs in at first light.

I'm sleepy, but I open my arms and she jumps into them.

"Daddy!" she shouts, bouncing. "Time to get up!"

"Mommy kept daddy awake last night, "I tell her. "Daddy's sleepy."

Zuzu glares at her mother. "Mommy, why did you do that? Daddy has to take me to the park!"

"I'm sure daddy will be fine," Mila promises her. "Go get dressed, pumpkin."

"Gabe is taking Eli, too," she tells me. "So you guys can go together. Maddy and I are going to go shopping for nursery furniture."

"No rest for the wicked, then," I roll my eyes as I climb out of bed.

"I thought it would be best to get right into a normal routine," she tells me worriedly. "Was that ok?"

I stop what I'm doing and come round the bed to her. I cup her face and make her look at me.

"Don't worry about trying to make life normal for me," I tell her firmly. "It's life. We can't always control it, but it will always be ours. We'll take it as it comes. But yes, I'm perfectly fine with going with Gabe to the park. Surely, between the two of us, we can control two children."

Mila smiles and kisses me sweetly, and I'm already looking forward to bedtime again. I tell her that.

"Me too," she admits.

"Let's meet here again tonight?" I suggest.

She nods. "It's a date."

"Let's make it a standing date," I add. "Say… for the next sixty years or so?"

Mila is radiant as she agrees. "I'll pencil you in," she says and I pull her to me, and all is right with the world.

"Use a permanent marker," I tell her and I kiss her until she's breathless.

"I almost forgot," she says, and she's flustered as she gets into the drawer of her nightstand. She pulls out something wrapped in tissue.

MY PEACE

"You know how Brand likes to make things out of leather?"

I nod.

"I asked him to make it for you. I didn't know if you'd wear it or not, but…" her voice trails off as I open it.

It's a leather bracelet. Words are stamped on it.

MY DEMONS DO NOT CONTROL ME.

"I thought it could be a reminder for you," she says hesitantly. "I mean, you probably don't need a reminder, but it never hurts, right?"

"It's perfect," I tell her as I snap it onto my wrist. "I'll wear it every day."

"You will?"

"I will," I nod. "Of course I will."

I follow her out of the bedroom and I glance at my wrist. The words stare back at me, wise and true.

My demons don't control me.

Not anymore.

I'm going to live a sober, healthy, happy life, surrounded by people I love.

I'm worth it.

Epilogue
Mila

Seven months later

Sometimes, I'm still jumpy in the night.

It's normal, they tell me. When a person has gone through what we did, with a person invading our home, it's impossible to not think of it at times.

I usually think of it in the night, when things go bump or shadows move on the walls.

We live in a gated community with a guard, and our home has a state of the art security system, so there is no reason to fear. We're more careful now, about the people we allow into our lives. We have to be.

I walk down the hall to the baby's room. "Shhhh, Ethan," I tell him, as I pick him up out of his crib. "It's ok, babe. It's ok."

I settle into the rocker nearby, and rock him as I nurse.

I hum a lullaby, and stare down at his sweet little face.

He already looks like Pax. He has his nose, his eyes. Even the cleft in his chin. I love that. I rock him, and hold him tight, and sing and sing, until his belly is finally full and he falls back to sleep in my arms.

His room is soothing and quiet, a calm green with cream colored furniture. It's perfect for a baby, and it's only steps from our own bedroom. I take a deep breath and inhale the honeysuckle scent. We'd had honeysuckle

MY PEACE

planted all around the house and it had taken root and grown like crazy. I must've left the window open earlier.

I tuck the baby back into his crib, and ponder the past few months.

Leroy had finally been tied to Natasha's crimes, and he will never taste freedom again. Pax has gone back to work, and he's still sober and strong. He goes to narcotics anonymous meetings, and he's still in therapy.

He's putting in the work.

We're happier than we've ever been, and now our little family is complete. Ethan sleeps peacefully in his crib as proof, his little hand curled up under his cheek.

I bend over the railing and kiss him on his head, inhaling his sweet smell.

There's nothing better than that smell.

I smile and head to the window to close it, only when I get there, it's already closed.

I'm confused for a minute, because the honeysuckle scent fills the room in a way that should happen only if the window was open.

But I'm tired, and maybe my olfactory senses are working overtime.

I pause at the door, and look back inside, and a feeling of such warmth and security and comfort comes over me that I close my eyes and just stand still, experiencing it with all of my might.

The warm feeling envelopes me, comforting me.
This is home.

I leave the door ajar, and return to bed where my husband waits.

About the Author

Courtney Cole is a New York Times and USA Today bestselling author who likes to write beneath palm trees at her home in Florida.

She is a wife, mom and novelist, but not necessarily in that order. She collects dashboard hula girls and is terrified of buoys and birds.

To learn more about her, visit
www.courtneycolewrites.com

Made in the USA
Coppell, TX
17 July 2021